Wish

Wish

JOSEPH MONNINGER

DELACORTE PRESS

All rights reserved. Published in the United States by Delacorte Press,
an imprint of Random House Children's Books, a division of
Random House, Inc., New York.

Delacorte Press is a registered trademark and
the colophon is a trademark of Random House, Inc.

Visit us on the Web! www.randomhouse.com/teens

Educators and librarians, for a variety of teaching tools,
visit us at www.randomhouse.com/teachers

Library of Congress Cataloging-in-Publication Data
Monninger, Joseph.
Wish / Joseph Monninger. — 1st ed.
Summary: While trying to help her eleven-year-old brother who suffers
from cystic fibrosis get his greatest wish, fifteen-year-old Bee discovers that
she has some special wishes of her own.
ISBN 978-0-385-73941-2 (hc : alk. paper) — ISBN 978-0-385-90788-0
(glb : alk. paper) — ISBN 978-0-375-89754-2 (ebook) [1. Brothers and
sisters—Fiction. 2. Cystic fibrosis—Fiction. 3. Wishes—Fiction.
4. Single-parent families—Fiction.] I. Title.
PZ7.M7537Wis 2010
[Fic]—dc22
2010009958

The text of this book is set in 12-point Cochin.

Book design by Marci Senders

Printed in the United States of America

10 9 8 7 6 5 4 3 2 1

First Edition

TO SANDEE AND CASEY BISSON

• • •

I believe implicitly that every young man in the world
is fascinated with either sharks or dinosaurs.
—Peter Benchley,
author of *Jaws*

There is no remedy for love, but to love more.
—Henry David Thoreau

• • •

WiSh

COLUMBUS DAY WEEKEND

FRIDAY

About an hour into the flight from New Hampshire to San Francisco the attendant came over and opened her eyes wide, like people sometimes do when they talk to friendly dogs, and said in a puffy way that she had just heard from my mom that we were heading out to California to see a great white shark, and wasn't that amazing, she had a cousin who was a diver and he had seen sharks, but never a great white, and weren't we scared, and she thought the cousin dove in the Caribbean, where was it, she couldn't remember, oh, yes, the Cayman Islands, did we know the Cayman Islands, and what kind of sharks did they have there?

"Black tips and reef sharks," Tommy, my brother, said with his short, breathy voice that made him sound like a little old man. "Maybe tigers and bulls, too. Definitely bulls."

I nodded and let him go sharky on her. Mainly, I had my eye on my mom, who had stopped about halfway up the aisle to speak to a guy in a business suit. Mom had her phony smile on, the one she uses when she meets men, and she wore the wide, hippie-dippie skirt that didn't really match the guy in the business suit. It was all wrong but she couldn't see that, *never* saw that, even though he probably pegged her for what she was—a woman too friendly to guys, a woman who would always stop in a plane aisle to say hello to a potential boyfriend. A woman who didn't notice the knot she made in foot traffic. A woman who tried to make things happen too fast.

That was our mom, Grace.

Grace Ouroussoff.

She had taken her maiden name back after our father left. He had been a furnace installer for the Dead River Company near our home in Warren, New Hampshire. I was four when he left and I don't remember much about him except that his hands smelled of glue, or solder, and he wore a Leatherman on his belt in a nylon holster that had a tiger embossed on its face. His name was Winterson. So it was Tommy Winterson and Bee (short for Beatrice) Winterson and my mother, who had reclaimed her Russian name. Only she didn't really look or act Russian. Her parents had been second-generation Russian, also partially Hungarian, and sometimes they served potato pancakes and crazy Russian food that consisted mostly of cabbage in different boiling vats, and they really, really liked Easter.

But on the plane, her right hip leaning against the passenger seat, her voice so high-pitched people couldn't help but watch, she flirted with Businessman Bob, tossing her head back and touching his shoulder. I doubted she would go out of her way to acknowledge our family connection, because that meant letting Businessman Bob know she had a fifteen-year-old daughter and an eleven-year-old son. It wouldn't take him long to do the math. Not to mention that most guys didn't think connecting with a woman with two kids was any sort of dream come true. Most guys ran the other way when they met us; then Mom would take to her bed with a roll of toilet paper, muttering that nothing mattered and that she hated her life, and complaining that she didn't deserve to be unhappy.

Up in the air, though, flying toward California, she was all smiles as she tossed her head back and laughed and Businessman Bob ordered little drinks in little bottles, and everyone passing them had to turn sideways to get by and people trying to sleep shook their heads and tried to find a comfortable position against their headrests.

• • •

Meanwhile, the attendant leaned against the rear of the seat in front of me and bent toward me. She had a ton of makeup on, swirls of it back by her ears, but she was pretty, too, in the kind of way a motel room might be pretty if you saw it in the right light. She smelled of moisturizer and perfume. I knew that all her chatter was meant to cover for my mom. In other words, she knew my mom wanted to chat up that guy, but she also seemed interested in the whole shark thing. Her name tag said *Charlene*.

"Your mom said this is your first flight," she said to me when Tommy finished bombarding her with shark facts. "For both of you? That's exciting."

"It's fun," I said. "So far so good."

"And you're in school, of course. How do you like it?"

"I like it okay," I said.

"I bet you're a good student."

"She's class president," Tommy said, which was not true exactly. I had been class president in ninth grade and was running for it this year. "She never even gets below an A-minus."

"Impressive! So are you thinking about college, Bee?"

I nodded. "I want to go to Dartmouth. It's in New Hampshire."

"She does the *New York Times* crossword puzzle every Sunday," Tommy said, enjoying putting me on the spot.

"And she writes for the school paper. And she can peel an apple in one continuous peel and do crow pose for about five minutes. That's a yoga position: you have to lift your whole body up and tilt forward and stay in a handstand."

"I know crow pose," Charlene said. "Wow, that's not easy."

"It's not that hard, either," I said, giving Tommy a look.

"Maybe for you," Charlene said. "I have trouble with downward dog. I'm just a beginner. Anyway, sounds as though you have a plan for your life, Bee."

"On the last day of school, Bee knew what she was wearing for the first day of school the following year," Tommy said. "I'm not kidding, either."

When she asked about Tommy, he gave her the little speech he had been giving since he heard from the Blue Moon program that he would be able to go into the water with great whites. A bunch of people who "mean well" find out about sick kids and they go to a lot of trouble to give the kid one big experience before the kid gets so weak and screwed up that he can't appreciate anything any longer. My mom applied on Tommy's behalf, and because she's a single mom, and because Tommy has cystic fibrosis, the foundation wrote right back. Then the local pastor, Reverend Pael, called to say he had been contacted to verify "our situation" and he had given the thumbs-up, which is the kind of phrase Reverend Pael uses because he's a dork and doesn't know it.

"Well, that's just terrific," Charlene said to Tommy and only partly to me. "That's just so exciting. But won't you be scared to get into the water with a great white?"

"I'll be in a dive cage," Tommy said.

"Still." Charlene pretended to shiver. "You're brave."

People always said that kind of thing to Tommy, as if saying he was brave or smart and daring somehow covered the fact that he had cystic fibrosis. They figured the teeter-totter had dipped so far down against him that they could put anything on the other side and he wouldn't notice it was phony. I simply nodded, trying to let Tommy have the limelight, but I also saw my mom writing down something on a piece of paper. She handed it to Businessman Bob and then looked down the aisle at me. She waved a little finger-scrunch wave. I scrunch-waved back.

TOMMY SHARK FACT #1: A great white will tilt its head out of the water so it can see seals on land or people on boats. It's the only shark known to exhibit this behavior.

● ● ●

Somewhere over the Rockies the plane started bouncing in turbulence. I suppose I had fallen asleep, because when I woke, Tommy had his head on my lap and his breathing was lousy. His face pointed toward the nose of the plane, so I couldn't see his expression, but his lungs sounded like a water pump looking for pressure. I listened, trying to gauge how bad he might be. His lungs routinely fill with mucus that is stickier than normal human mucus. It makes his lungs perfect for breeding bacteria, and it makes it almost impossible to clear them. I couldn't remember a time his lungs didn't sound as though they were searching for something they could never find.

The plane lights had dimmed and when I looked at the seat in front of us I didn't see my mother. I leaned into the aisle to see if she had slid in beside the businessman, but I couldn't see her there, either. The plane took a nice bump, one of those shuddery kinds of things that make you wonder if your belly has a bottom, and Tommy lifted up from my lap, a glistening string of drool running like a silver scar on his right cheek.

He shook his head at me and looked in my eyes.

That meant he couldn't breathe.

"Use your inhalant," I said.

He shook his head again.

It meant he had misplaced it. He always misplaced his inhalant. He was eleven and he lost everything you handed to him.

I reached into my pocket and pulled out the one I always

kept on me. *Pulmozyme*. To make his sputum less sticky. I had a dozen stashed around the house, but I always had one in my pocket for him. Sometimes I worried he depended on me too much for the inhalant because he knew I would cover him. But he still had to have the stuff one way or the other.

"Here," I said.

He tilted it into his mouth, pressed down, breathed in. The plane dipped and shuddered again. He coughed a quick, ugly cough, then breathed three times fast through his nose. He nodded and inhaled off the Pulmozyme again. The plane steadied. I studied him.

"Better?" I asked.

He nodded.

"Clear?" I asked.

"Pretty clear," he said. "Thanks, Bee."

I stood and fished around in the overhead for his vest. He has to wear a special vest at least twice a day. It massages and shakes his chest, loosening the mucus. It's gross to think about, but gross doesn't really figure into it when you're around Tommy for long. Either you take care of him or he dies.

I helped him slide into the vest, Velcroed it shut, then turned it on. It made a buzzing sound like the sound of a hair dryer as it's turning off. But it never turned off. It just kept going. The vest cost about ten grand. My mother always mentions the price to impress people. But she didn't pay for it. Her wages from her job as a hostess at the Morningside Restaurant in Bristol didn't come close to buying a ten-thousand-dollar vest. It was welfare, or Medicaid, or some government program for sick kids that covered the expense.

I sat and watched Tommy for a minute to make sure the vest worked properly. I tried to imagine what it must be like to know you needed your lungs shaken just to breathe. Whenever he wore the vest he looked straight ahead, his eyes focused on nothing, his arms out as if he wanted to block someone from coming through a door. As if he wanted to tell the whole world to step back. I wondered if he felt his lungs loosening, or if he felt like a snow globe, his liquids jostling and moving until he could be still again.

TOMMY SHARK FACT #2: Female whites grow larger than males. No one is quite sure why. Whites hunt mammals, seals, and sea lions primarily. Whites—also called pointers in Australia—patrol like sentries near seal colonies. When the seals take to the water, the sharks swim beneath them, waiting and gauging the right time to attack. Like most predators, sharks ambush their prey. Their coloring is darker on top so that they blend into the ocean floor. When they rise, or breach, they come full force to the surface and hit a seal with the impact of a truck. Usually they inflict one lethal bite. Frequently they decapitate the seal and leave it to bleed like a punctured tube of paint into the water. That's when the whites circle, giving a classic fin-cleaving-the-water show that people both love and hate to watch. They devour the seal in a few bites once it has ceased struggling. Blood spreads on the water and gulls dive in to get scraps of flesh.

● ● ●

My mother says Tommy's fascination with sharks is really a fascination with his disease. She says Tommy sees himself as the seal, and the shark as the quick bright thing coming up from the sea bottom. Sometimes I like Mom's metaphors; other times they seem like pure rot. Tommy doesn't have a metaphoric shark in his chest. He has a clogged filter, but Mom doesn't like seeing it that way.

Dad was the practical one, I guess. He could fix anything and people always called him on the weekends to do quick chores. He never charged his friends, which drove my mother crazy. If you study pictures of him, he looks like one sort of person on a Sunday—cleaned up and a little uncomfortable in his decent clothes—and another sort of person the rest of the week. Mostly he wore a blue coverall and a Boston Red Sox baseball hat. He whistled, too. I liked hearing him whistle and it's one of my only memories of him. He whistled sharp and you heard him coming and going, his truck banging around with tools, his keys jingling, his boots solid on the floor. Mom might float away, but Dad stayed anchored. Now and then I hear a man whistle and I think, Maybe that's Dad, but it never is. Mom thinks he went to Florida, which is a strange place for a furnace installer to go.

Mr. Cotter, the point person for Blue Moon, met us at the San Francisco airport.

He looked to be about a thousand years old, until you checked his eyes, which were bright blue and alert, like a swimming pool on a hot day. He wore a grandpa hat, a kind of brimmed straw thing, and his shirt opened a little near his chest. I saw his T-shirt, a wifebeater, and dog tags. He had a baseball hat for Tommy. A shark fin stuck up from the top of the hat, and when I glanced at Tommy, I knew it broke his heart. He hated people turning his shark interest into something stupid and gory, but Mom grabbed the hat as soon as she saw it and popped it on Tommy's head. He looked like an idiot. I'm not sure why, but my eyes filled seeing him like that, and I had to look away, because at last the kid was where he wanted to be, a kid who couldn't breathe a decent breath his entire life, and in this one moment of pure happiness he had to put on a stupid hat that cheapened everything. Mr. Cotter hadn't meant anything wrong by it—he probably thought he was being lighthearted and fun, and Tommy, a frail boy who weighed less than eighty pounds and whose chest stayed packed with mud and puke half the time, thanked Mr. Cotter politely and wore the hat like a champ.

"You folks excited?" Mr. Cotter asked.

"Oh, yes," Mom said. "This is all we've been talking about for a month at least."

"Well, we have quite a trip lined up for you," Mr. Cotter said, leading us away from the baggage claim the way old guys do, his hand out as if showing you a fine carpet. "The weather is supposed to be clear tomorrow, so the captain thinks we should have a good day. You'll be with a group, some other kids, so it should be fun."

"What other kids?" Tommy asked.

"Oh, another group of shark lovers. You'll see."

I knew right then that it wasn't going to be what Tommy wanted it to be. And I knew he knew. As I watched him walking, his shark hat bobbing above his blue backpack, I put my hand on his shoulder. He looked up at me and smiled. I felt close to crying again, and I wanted to tell everyone to stop, just stop, that we couldn't mess up this kid's one dream by turning it into an ugly Disney outing.

That wasn't what Tommy wanted. But Tommy would never say anything. He had endured too much in his life, expected too little, and he would go along with whatever happened.

I looked at my mother. She glanced at me and smiled. She had reapplied her lipstick as we landed, and she glowed from the sense of travel and adventure, and from having an expense account for a four-day stay in California. The last thing in the world she wanted was anyone rocking the boat and she deliberately looked away from me, stepping up a little to be beside Mr. Cotter, her swirling skirt floating on the warm California air. As far as she was concerned, we were on vacation, and we were a family who hadn't been on a vacation ever, not once, and probably wouldn't be again for years to come.

Mr. Cotter led us outside to an enormous black Cadillac parked in the Arrivals section. The car looked to be about twenty years old, but in mint condition. We threw our bags in the humongous trunk. Mom sat up front, mildly flirting even with a geezer like Mr. Cotter, and I sat in back with Tommy. Mom said she had been in California years ago, but only to San Diego, south of here, and blah blah blah.

I looked at Tommy. He seemed exhausted, worn out

from the flight, but he leaned forward expectantly, as if he wanted to see every last thing around him. Mr. Cotter explained that we had a room on Fisherman's Wharf, and then asked if Tommy knew anything about Joe DiMaggio. Joe D, as Mr. Cotter called him, had been a native San Franciscan and had played for the Seals, a minor-league team, before moving on to the Yankees. Mr. Cotter might have been talking about Santa Claus for all the reality it had for Tommy, but Tommy nodded and said it was interesting.

Then we had that quiet that sometimes comes over a carload of people. I've experienced it before. Everyone is tired, and no one has anything new to say, and so for a few minutes you simply ride along, your head leaning against the window. I had no idea where we were, or where we were going, but Mr. Cotter drove calmly and I felt peaceful and empty and good. I reached over and held Tommy's hand.

When we got to the hotel—the Hyatt on Fisherman's Wharf—my mother casually asked where Oakland was in relation to the hotel. My body was half in the car and half out, and it took me about a second to know the score. Obviously, Businessman Bob had been from Oakland. She tried to phrase it casually, as if she happened to be a geography bug and simply wanted to get her bearings, and Mr. Cotter fell for it. Old men love to talk about directions, and I almost laughed because he gave her more than she bargained for. Meanwhile, I grabbed our bags and stacked them by the door, where a bellhop began putting them on a luggage trolley. I didn't know if we were supposed to have that kind of service, if the Blue Moon agreement covered tips and things, but I didn't stop the guy. By the time Mr. Cotter finished explaining the directions to Oakland, the bellhop had us ready to go into the hotel.

"Mom," I said, to peel her away, "I think Tommy's tired."

She nodded. She was tired, too. We all were.

Mr. Cotter took the cue. He told us he would pick us up at five the next morning. He handed Mom an envelope to "cover incidentals." Then he patted Tommy on the shoulder and went back around the front of the Cadillac. He waved one last time and climbed inside, and a second later his Cadillac floated away from the curb.

I helped Tommy write his Blue Moon Foundation application.

Mrs. Burns, his English teacher at Pemigewasset Junior High, helped him with the final draft. The grammar and form are better than Tommy could do by himself, but it sounds like Tommy anyway.

I have CF—cystic fibrosis.

Twice a day (at least) I wear a vest that massages and shakes my chest, and usually I feel better afterward, but not always.

I have some digestive problems, too, a deficiency with my pancreas. My body does not absorb the fat from foods the way other people's bodies do, so I take an enzyme-replacement capsule with each meal. I take vitamins A and D, because I'm always low on those, but I still never put on weight. I'm skinny, and bony, and my head looks too big on my shoulders. I'm not saying that for sympathy. I've looked at myself enough in the mirror and I know it's true. I look a little like an alien, especially because I have big eyes, and kids called me Froggy when I was younger, but the teachers made them stop that. Some kids called me E.T.

The long and short of it is, I am undersized, and I have to be careful with certain foods, like dairy, that increase the production of phlegm. The big deal is that my life expectancy is shorter than the average person's by almost half. I should live to about my mid-thirties or early forties, and I am eleven now, so I am nearly a third finished with my life. Also, it's uncertain if I can have children, because CF affects fertility. Even if I can have children, some experts feel carriers should not risk passing along the gene. Each cell in our bodies contains twenty-two pairs of chromosomes and one pair of sex chromosomes. The faulty gene that causes CF is found on chromosome 7. About one in twenty-two people have the CF mutation on one of the pair of number 7 chromosomes, and those people are called carriers. They have no symptoms of CF. When both parents are CF carriers, a child has a one-in-four chance of being born with CF, a one-in-two chance of being a carrier, and a one-in-four chance of being healthy.

The Blue Moon Foundation is one of the best things going in the lives of kids like me. It gives us hope. I would like to go and dive with great white sharks because they are the apex predator fish and they fascinate me. Although I love *Jaws* and Shark Week and all the sensational elements associated with sharks, I also love the biology of sharks. They are one of the oldest organisms on earth and I am one of the youngest, so I have a great deal to learn from them. When a shark swims the seas, he is also swimming in time. I suppose we all are, but sharks have done it longer.

I live with my mother, Grace, and my sister, Beatrice, in Warren, New Hampshire. My mother is a single mom. My sister takes care of me a lot and she is an honor student and class president at Woodsville High School. I attend Pemigewasset Junior High and I average in the B range because I miss plenty of school when things with my CF kick in. I'm not making excuses, it's just a fact of life. In my free time, I surf the Web, mostly in shark chat communities.

If I were to be in the ocean with a shark—a great white off the coast of California—it would be my ultimate dream. I hope you will consider my application. I'm sure there are many kids worse off than I am, so I will understand if you cannot fund my wish.

Some observations about Fisherman's Wharf.

1. It's a tourist trap.
2. If you're in San Francisco, you kind of have to go. Everything in San Francisco points back to Fisherman's Wharf. Probably because it isn't hilly like the rest of the city and you can smell the ocean. Portland, Maine, has a wharf sort of like it, but it's much smaller and not nearly such a big deal.
3. It's a wharf, which means boats dock there, and fishermen push carts around and people throw fish and shout. They do

it for the tourists, but they also do it for real, sort of. It's kind of half and half.

4. You could spend a billion dollars on clothes in the shops. Anything you've seen in fashion magazines is here—way more than in all of New Hampshire. It's all supertrendy and people walk around with smoothies and crazy coffees and shop. That's all anyone seems to do on Fisherman's Wharf. Plus eat.

5. I bet some nights it's easy to get jammed into a crowd, with people pushing and trying to get by one another. But October seems calmer. You can't really see the stars except way out at the horizon where the city lights don't penetrate.

6. About a million kids roam around, most of them skateboarders. It's like seeing the edge of an entire street culture rubbing up against the tourists.

7. The brochures say you can eat excellent Chinese food, but we didn't find any.

8. It's three thousand miles away from New Hampshire.

9. It's made of wood and people get splinters, but a lot of kids go barefoot anyway. Stupid.

10. It reminds me of fairs we have in New Hampshire in the fall. It smells like french fries and fried dough, only they have different things here like deep-fried cheese curds.

11. The sun sets in the ocean here and in the mountains in New Hampshire. We once went to Cadillac Mountain, Maine, which is supposed to be the first place the sun strikes land in the lower forty-eight states. It's weird to think of the sun traveling all the way across the states and landing in the ocean

right here. I know the sun doesn't really travel—I mean, we spin, and the sun moves, and all that—but the East Coast is the golf tee and this is the hole.

Mom bought us dinner at a crab stand. The brochure from the hotel claimed that Fisherman's Wharf crab stands constituted the raison d'être—or "reason for being"—for the area. Originally people came for the crabs and the local flavor of the fishing fleet. Eventually the spot became a tourist destination. Now you can take boat rides and sail under the Golden Gate Bridge, or take a trip to Alcatraz, the famous prison. If you hold a dollar in the air, ten people will help you spend it.

We ate at the crab booth, sitting on stools. It was nice being outside on a fall night. Mom was in a good mood. We had money for once—she showed me the envelope Mr. Cotter had given her, which contained a thousand dollars in twenty-dollar bills—and we actually behaved like a family, sort of. Tommy looked happy. He didn't say anything about the other kids scheduled to be on the boat with him, or what it might mean for his chances to dive with a great white. He concentrated on the crabs and french fries and his orange soda, and I could almost see his lungs relaxing a little in the salt air.

I felt good, too. School seemed a million miles away. New Hampshire in October is beautiful, all the leaves turning and woodstoves beginning to push smoke up the chimneys, but on Fisherman's Wharf you could see every kind of person, and people looked happy to be on vacation, or killing time, and living felt easier somehow. I thought of my friends, Jill and Marcie and Maggie, but I'd left my cell phone at home on purpose so that I wouldn't be tempted to text them. This trip was for Tommy and I had pledged not to divide my attention. I didn't want to start obsessing about schoolwork, or the lame social scene at Woodsville High, or about any of the half dozen idiotic boys who hung around us. It didn't matter right then. I pulled my sweater tighter around my shoulders and breathed, really breathed, for what felt like the first time in months. I knew I carried tension in my shoulders, so I straightened them and worked on my posture. I drank my soda down to the ice and made a cross-eyed face that often got Tommy laughing. It was supposed to mean that we had sucked in so far that our eyes bent inward. Or it could mean that we had sucked down something cold and we had an ice headache, something we called a caveman, because all you could do when you had one was make stupid grunting sounds, like *uhhh uhhh uhhh*. I looked over at Tommy and expected him to laugh, but instead he put his hand up for quiet and turned his head.

In that instant, Tommy heard them.

"Seals," Tommy said.

He stood and started walking.

I had never seen him move more quickly, or with such determination. Mom had the same reaction as I did, because she called out to him, trying to get him to wait, but he didn't pay any attention. Luckily Mom had already settled the bill, so I hustled after him with Mom trailing me. Tommy didn't acknowledge our existence. I listened to the noise that had attracted him, an *arrrr arrrr arrrrr* that could only have been made by seals, but I'm not sure I would have noticed it without him. Tommy lifted his head and I realized that he usually walked hunched over, his lungs a stubborn weight in his chest, his legs underdeveloped, but suddenly he shucked out of that. He was *on point,* as my uncle Louis said about bird dogs when they struck a trail.

Tommy didn't say *There* or *Look* or turn to see if we had followed when he arrived at the overlook of Pier 39. He simply stopped at the metal railing and let his eyes run all over the sight before him.

As soon as I saw the sea lions stretched out on the docks, their bodies like so many shrugs of meat, I remembered seeing the same scene on TV programs, and on postcards, but I hadn't really considered that it existed in a place and time and that I could visit it. Sea lions lounged everywhere, their bodies scattered and limp, their fur glossy and brilliant. Two sea lions, maybe males, had squared off and now barked furiously at each other, while a few seals answered tentatively from another dock. Cameras flashed all around the seals and people raised their hands and pointed at this one or that one. Tommy simply watched.

"Oh, the seals!" Mom said when we had collected at the railing overlooking the pier. "Tommy, don't run off like that again."

He nodded.

Mom dug in her purse for the digital camera she had borrowed from Aunt Carol. It took her a second to get the camera out, figure how to work it, and point it. When she felt comfortable with it, she told us to turn so that she could take our photograph. She wanted to have the seals in the background, and she thought if she got up on her toes she might be able to catch the right angle.

I turned.

Tommy didn't.

"Tommy?" she said.

He didn't respond.

"Tommy?" she asked again.

He shook his head.

Mom looked at me. I shrugged. Tommy refused to budge. She made a small half circle to try to get his profile, but he shaded his body away and continued to look. I guessed that he had taken the shark hat and worn it like a good sport, and he had accepted the news that other kids might be on the shark boat tomorrow, all without protest. But now the seals lay right in front of him, the real animals, his sharks' favorite food, and no one on earth was going to interfere with that. He didn't have to say it for me to know it. He didn't want to be rude to Mom, but he also didn't want the trip to become a big snapshot of family fun. And because he had trouble expressing himself, because he was Tommy, he had reacted the only way he could. He had finally reached his sharks' world, and though it's probably crazy to care so much about something that you refuse to undermine it even in the smallest way, he did and I admired the heck out of him for that.

Mom fussed a second and said she didn't know why he was being so difficult, and then she gave up. She looked at the seals for a few minutes, making small observations and oohing a little when they did something cute. After a while she told us she needed a cup of coffee and that she would be right back. I watched her go, then turned to Tommy.

"Tell me about them," I whispered.

He let me take his hand.

"The males weigh about eight hundred pounds," he said, his voice flat and sure in a way I had rarely heard it before, "and the females are a lot smaller. They live up and down the West Coast. They can swim almost twenty-five miles an hour. They raft together and play when they feel like it. I'm not sure if they can close their ears when they dive, but

I think they do. They eat rockfish and hake and other ground stockfish. And they eat small fish on the fly, I guess, and squid. Their scientific name is *Zalophus californianus*."

I'm not sure why but my eyes started to tear. What a nutty kid to know all this. How many hours, I wondered, had he waited for this moment?

"And the sharks?" I asked, still quiet.

"They could be right out there," he said, pointing with his chin. "Where we're going tomorrow isn't far from here. The sharks patrol colonies like these and pick off the young ones or even one of the large males. Scientists just started tracking the great whites' winter migration. But scientists know the whites come here in the fall. This is an old meeting place. Like for a thousand years."

"Do the seals know the whites are out there waiting for them?"

He nodded. We watched for a while. Not many people looking down at the pier, I figured, had thought about the sharks waiting for the seals to slide into their strike zone.

"I don't know if the seals have memory, if that's what you mean," Tommy said after a bit. "They know it's dangerous to enter the water, but they have to eat. Whites ambush them. It's the way it works. It's all done in shadows, with the water kind of hard to see through. Things flash around and then suddenly they collide."

"Do you feel sorry for the seals?" I asked.

"Yes and no. Marine parks use sea lions in their water shows. They're smart. They can balance a ball on their nose, but nobody really knows why they can do that. The sharks have to be huge to attack them. Leopard seals kill penguins around the South Pole and domestic cats kill robins. It's just the way nature does things."

"Is there usually more than one shark?"

He shrugged.

"There could be a dozen patrolling. Maybe more. It's seasonal. But they used to say that if you escaped Alcatraz and tried to swim for it, the sharks would get you."

We didn't talk after that. I listened to the water and the sea lions barking. And I thought about the great whites surfacing on a dark night to watch the land with their black eyes, judging the moment when the seals would slide in and join them.

That night, back in the hotel, Tommy phoned Ty Barry.

Ty Barry was Tommy's hero, because Ty Barry had survived a great white attack near Mavericks in Northern California. Mavericks was a spot about a half mile out to sea with a famous break for surfing. Tommy had e-mailed Ty shortly after he read the story in the newspaper and never expected a reply. But Ty Barry had e-mailed back, telling the details as best he could. They continued to write back and forth, and I always wondered if Ty knew about Tommy's condition, or if he simply liked an insane kid who e-mailed out of the blue to get the inside shark story. In the end, it didn't matter. Ty put Tommy in touch with a bunch of other surfers with shark stories. Tommy gobbled those stories up. I never read any of the correspondence, but Tommy always had a new shark tale.

Ty Barry's story went like this:

Ty had been paddling on his surfboard about a half mile from shore when a shark smashed him from underneath and tossed him eight feet into the air. Ty didn't really know what had happened. Fortunately, neither his arms nor his legs had been in the water, and the shark managed to hit the board perfectly, leaving gigantic teeth marks in the foam core but missing Ty entirely. Ty had been tethered at the ankle to the board, and for a second he debated whether he should climb back on or swim for it. He couldn't spot the shark. A surfer friend nearby shouted to him, asking if that had been a shark. Ty shouted back that it sure as hell was, then he climbed back onto his board. As soon as he slid his belly onto the surface of the board, he happened to look down and see the shark swim directly underneath. It all happened so fast, he couldn't say with certainty what length the shark was, but the teeth gouges led experts to determine that the white had been at least fifteen feet and weighed maybe a ton or more.

Ty Barry and his friend paddled the entire way back to shore expecting to be attacked by the shark again. But the shark had disappeared.

Ty Barry said the only thing he felt the instant before the impact was a blister of water surging up from the bottom. A bullet inside a wave, sort of.

According to Tommy, Ty also said that the chances of a great white hitting you on a surfboard were maybe one in a million. For a shark to hit your board and *not* touch you had to be one in a trillion. He imagined it had to be similar to walking through the jungle while carrying an ironing board in front of you, and having a tiger jump out of the undergrowth and hit just the ironing board, then take off without touching you. He said that had been his experience with the shark.

Ty Barry meant more to Tommy than anything except sharks. In most ways that counted, Ty Barry was Tommy's only friend.

After Tommy called Ty Barry, Mom got a call from the guy on the plane: Businessman Bob. I realized, watching her, that she had known it was coming, because she snatched up her cell phone right away and turned her back so that we wouldn't see her expression.

I hated her guts for expecting a call from him. I hated her guts for giving out her number. I didn't know for sure, but I suspected that she had talked to him while Tommy and I looked at the seals, and that the coffee search had simply been her phony excuse to get away from us. I cringed as her voice got airy and flirty, giving guys the impression that she's some dizzy idiot chick who believes the world revolves around them. She had changed into a pair of pajama bottoms and a hooded sweatshirt (it said *Jelly-stone Park* on it and had a small picture of Yogi Bear on the right sleeve), and she had three kernels of Smartfood cheese popcorn in her left hand, halfway to her mouth, and she put the popcorn down slowly so he wouldn't hear her mowing her big mouth, and she said, "Jerrod, how are you?"

Gag.

She talked for a second, her voice getting bright, and I happened to look at Tommy. He stared straight ahead at the TV—a monster truck thing that he had found—and I saw the color rise in his face. You didn't have to be Sigmund Freud to understand what he felt, or thought. His mom had scooped a guy on the plane, and now she was compromising the shark trip by turning her focus away from our half-baked family night. And you could tell

Tommy wondered why she had to flirt that night, why it was so important, and I felt the same way, so when she glanced at where we sat on the bed I pointed to the bathroom and made her go in there. That hardly helped, because her voice cut through the walls and it sounded even worse, almost as if she had a lover in there with her and they were laughing and kissing and cooing. Eventually Tommy pointed the remote at the TV and blasted the volume up so that all you could hear was Big Daddy Dan driving his crushing big-tire truck over the bodies of a bunch of beat-up sedans. Then Tommy pointed the remote at the bathroom and pretended to turn the volume down. In other words, he muted our mother. It was pretty funny, and I started to laugh. We both did.

"That was Jerrod," Mom said when she came out of the bathroom ten minutes later. She was all jazzed up. Someone had paid attention to her.

"What flavor is Jerrod?" Tommy asked, his eyes still on the television.

My mother stopped dead.

"What did you say, young man?" she asked.

He didn't answer.

She walked over and turned down the television. She crossed her arms over her chest. Tommy raised the remote and shot her.

The sound went up behind her.

"Tommy?" she asked. "What did you say, young man?"

She turned down the volume again. He turned it up.

I couldn't help laughing.

Then we had a good moment. For just a second I saw the Angry Mom swing in behind her eyes, but then she left. Instead Normal Mom smiled and pretended to go for the volume a third time, and Tommy turned the television all the way off. When she took a step away, he turned it back on. Mom smiled again. For once it was a really good smile, an ear-to-ear grin, and she looked young for a second, carefree, and you had to smile back watching her. Part of me knew she played around to kind of smooth out the business about getting a call from Jerrod, and part of me knew she was making things up to Tommy, but another part of me knew that life wasn't always easy for her. She had figured a way to get Tommy to California so that he could look at sharks. I had to give her credit for that. Besides, it was hard to be mad at her when she stood in front of our two beds and goofed around. Tommy called out that she should shing-a-ling, which was part of an old game we used to play: you called out a dance and Mom had to do it. Dance jukebox, we called it. Some nights we went crazy at it in the kitchen, but that was years ago.

She didn't hesitate, which is what is good about my Mom. As soon as Tommy shouted "Shing-a-ling," she started hamming it up, dancing this corny sixties dance, prancing and moving her hands up and down.

"The monkey," I called and she did that, too, monkeying like a maniac, then switching into the mashed potato when Tommy told her to, and Mom went extra-wild, goofy, smearing everything right into a version of the hustle and the shopping cart, and the water sprinkler. She did a go-go move with her legs pumping up and down for a few seconds, and she swung her arms around and up and down as if she wanted to pound her fists on a big drum, then she brought her hands across her eyes to do the Batman. She made an awful noise clunking around. Sometimes her knees creaked and cracked and that made us call out more dances, trying to get her to cave. Afterward we made her rap, throwing out topics that she had to rhyme and look "street" about. It was all absurd and pretty hilarious.

I looked at Tommy, who was laughing as hard as I had seen him laugh in a long time. And maybe wishes weren't something you hoped for, but instead something that found you. Tommy, Mom, and I were three specks in a big world, I thought, with sharks in the seas around us.

SATURDAY

The smell of the ocean is always new. You could be away from it for a hundred years, or live by it every day, and when the wind finally brings the ocean's scent to you, you recognize it deep down somewhere. My first smell of the Pacific came on the wharf when we watched the seals, but at 5:23 the next morning from the backseat of Mr. Cotter's Cadillac I smelled it again and it was new. Mr. Cotter had showed up at five precisely, his legs covered by a pair of wind pants, his nose marked by a dot of zinc oxide, a blue fleece buttoned up around his chin. He brought a coffee thermos and a half gallon of orange juice and a box of

Dunkin' Donuts muffins and bagels. He didn't mention that Tommy forgot to wear the shark hat or even that Mom made us all wait fifteen minutes while she showered. He fixed us a little place to eat on the top of a cooler he had in his car trunk while we waited for Mom, and Tommy and I ate there while we watched the sun come up and felt the morning wind die away.

I had to hand it to Mr. Cotter: he figured out how Tommy wanted to take the shark trip. He didn't keep making jokes, or plying Tommy with questions about sharks devouring things, and while we ate he talked quietly about his own experience with the sea, and how he sailed sometimes in a small boat, and how he grew up in Northern California but had gone to school back East, to Dartmouth, actually, which was why he took a special interest in Tommy's application. That brought New Hampshire into the conversation, and he asked us where we lived, how far into the White Mountains, if we hiked up in Mount Moosilauke — he had fished the Baker River there while he attended Dartmouth — and if we ate maple syrup on snow in the spring. Turns out he had retired as a radiologist, his wife had died, and his children, all grown, lived near him. He enjoyed competitive croquet, and played most afternoons with a bunch of old fogeys (his word) on a court on an acre of land they bought together for that purpose.

"Bee wants to go to Dartmouth," Tommy said at one

point. "She goes over to the campus and walks around and pretends she's a student there."

I bumped Tommy's shoulder and turned red.

"Is that so, Bee?" Mr. Cotter asked. "It's a great school."

"It's my top choice," I said.

"She wants to go to the Ivy League," Tommy said, crumbs from his blueberry muffin flecking his chest. "And she will. Whatever Bee sets her mind to, she does."

"That's an admirable trait," Mr. Cotter said, looking at me as if for the first time. "Be sure you get in touch with me when you get ready to apply. I pull a little bit of weight out there."

"I will," I said. "Thanks."

Mr. Cotter and I exchanged a look, then we went back to eating bagels. I sipped coffee. It tasted smooth and rich.

Afterward, Mr. Cotter talked about volunteering for the Blue Moon Foundation, which he had been doing for three or four years, he couldn't remember exactly. Tommy said, "Thank you, Mr. Cotter," and Mr. Cotter reached out a hand and put it on Tommy's shoulder and I knew Mr. Cotter understood that Tommy had a difficult ride with CF, and that the purpose of the trip couldn't be separated from the reality of Tommy's shortened life. Mr. Cotter didn't have to say much, and neither did Tommy. Mr. Cotter patted Tommy's shoulder twice, then went back to his coffee.

Finally Mom showed up, a big tote bag at her side, her hair pulled back in a nutty-looking ponytail, her body trailing too much perfume. She grabbed a muffin, apologized for making us wait, and laughed when Mr. Cotter said the tides wait for no man but they will for a woman. Then we climbed into the Cadillac and drove toward the pier.

That's how the ocean found us.

TOMMY SHARK FACT #3: When most people think of a great white, they usually think in terms of length. That's a mistake, according to Tommy. A great white's girth is its most extraordinary feature. A nineteen-foot great white could take a six-foot-tall human and swallow him like a sideways Ritz cracker. Great whites are wide, and round, and come through the water like a moving tunnel. Peter Benchley, the author of *Jaws*, wrote: "Sharks have no interest in hurting you; they just want to eat you."

● ● ●

Captain O'Shay told us to come aboard the *Gray Jay*.

He was a big man with a big boat. He wore a Giants hat and a Giants hoodie and his boat had a Giants insignia painted on the hull. Something had happened to his face a long time ago, because his left profile appeared dented, as if someone had started to remold his features and then lost interest. He hadn't shaved in a while, and his cheek whiskers appeared white when you looked at him in a certain light. His voice carried to an unusual degree, as if he had spent his life shouting over the wind and could no longer remember what it was to speak quietly.

"It's a little snotty out on the water," he said by way of welcome, "but we should be okay. Three attacks on elephant seals yesterday. Welcome aboard. Welcome. Mind your step."

"Hello, Dave," Mr. Cotter said, handing the captain the cooler. "You're looking well."

"Henry, you old salt," Captain O'Shay called back.

Obviously, they knew each other.

Before we had climbed completely aboard, a short yellow school bus pulled in at the top of the pier. I felt my stomach sink. The bus made a beeping sound as it backed into a parking slot. I didn't turn to look at Tommy, but I knew he had spotted it. I stepped on board behind my mom. She held her hand out to Captain O'Shay. He smiled and shook it. A pair of gulls laughed right then. The birds lifted into the air and slid sideways on the wind.

"So, you must be Tommy," Captain O'Shay said to my brother in his loud, kettle voice. "Well, we should have a good day. As I said, three attacks yesterday. This time of year, you can usually depend on at least one a day, but you never know. Sometimes you get five. That's the record, anyway."

"Off Indian Head?" Tommy asked.

The captain looked carefully at him. I had seen it happen before. People dismissed Tommy as a cute little CF kid, but then Tommy said something that changed their perception. I saw Captain O'Shay reappraise him.

"You know the islands?" he asked Tommy.

"Just from studying them. Shark Alley, Mirounga Bay, North Landing. Just some of the places."

Captain O'Shay looked at Mr. Cotter, then back to Tommy.

Before the captain could say anything else, the bus began to unload.

Challenged kids.

You could tell right away. A large lady holding a clipboard climbed down first, then leaned inside and said something to the group. It took her a long time to say what she needed to say. When she pulled back out, it was almost as if the suction of her body leaving the door yanked the kids free from the bus. They stepped down haltingly, forming in loose pairs, and then started pointing at the boat. Their voices came pretty hard over the salt air, and the modulations were all wrong, too high, too wild. A couple of the kids started charging down the gangway to the boat and the large lady swooped after them.

I couldn't breathe, watching them.

And I didn't dare look at Tommy.

Because Tommy was not a kid who was challenged in that particular way. And I would never, ever say anything against those kids, but it wasn't fair for Tommy to be lumped in with them. I imagined right away how it all went: how Mr. Cotter, or maybe another well-meaning grown-up at the foundation, had contacted Captain O'Shay and booked the boat for a group rate. Maybe they had dickered over the price, appealing to O'Shay's sense of philanthropy, and I could guess the reasoning. They were all kids and they all had impairments. Tommy was simply one more kid, and the grown-ups didn't mean anything bad by it, but that's what it was. I glanced at Mr. Cotter and saw his face clouding over, because now, I knew, he understood Tommy better. Tommy probably knew more about sharks than anyone on the boat, but he was relegated to being a plain tourist, a kid, and he didn't deserve that.

It also pained me to see that Tommy understood one more thing. Once and for all he realized that people regarded him as they regarded the kids getting off the bus. Different. Less, somehow. Needful.

● ● ●

The large lady's name was Mrs. Halpern.

She had a smaller, younger woman with her, Ms. Sprague, as a second-in-command. Mrs. Halpern was in charge, but Ms. Sprague did the legwork. They reminded me of two dogs herding the kids down the gangway. Mrs. Halpern was a big, slow-moving guard dog; Ms. Sprague was a border collie, quick to move, quick to react.

Mrs. Halpern introduced the kids, but I didn't really listen. Maybe that sounds unfair, or mean-spirited, but I didn't care. They took a while to navigate the gangplank, to slip into life jackets, to adjust themselves to the boat's rocking. I had nothing against them. One, a girl, turned to me and said something about sharks, and about the ocean, and I nodded. Another pointed at some gulls.

And when a boy of about ten got his arm tangled in the life vest, Tommy stepped nearer and helped him.

I felt all my anger drain away. I watched Tommy move forward, his step as weak as some of the challenged kids, and I saw him meet the boy's eyes. The boy clearly had motor-skill difficulties, but he smiled as Tommy helped him straighten the jacket and pull it tight. And Tommy, his small, unhealthy body unsteady on the rolling boat, did not exhibit a moment's hesitation at touching a stranger. He moved with gentle deliberateness, his attention transferred to his fingers as he straightened the jacket. He patted the boy's shoulder.

"I'm Tommy," Tommy introduced himself. "You're Mark?"

"Mark," the boy said, though his voice garbled the name a little.

"Okay," Tommy said. "Let's have a good day."

That simple.

TOMMY SHARK FACT #4: Pliny the Elder, in AD 78, wrote that fossilized sharks' teeth rained from the sky during lunar eclipses. Other writers of the time speculated that the teeth were actually serpent tongues turned to stone by St. Peter. The teeth became known as *glossopetrae* — "tongue stones" — which possessed magical powers. People wore them as amulets and tailors sewed special pockets in garments so that the *glossopetrae* could be kept close to the body. Not until the mid-seventeenth century did a Danish scientist named Steno dissect a great white's head from an animal captured off the coast of Italy. Eventually the shark's teeth figured into its Latin name, *Carcharodon carcharias*, or "ragged tooth."

● ● ●

We passed under the Golden Gate Bridge, which was beautiful, but dangerous, according to Mr. Cotter. He said people looked out from San Francisco and saw a clear day and made the mistake of assuming the whole ocean was a pond. Once they hit the Golden Gate Bridge, things changed rapidly, and suddenly the ocean became an ocean. Add fog and a ton of tricky currents, and the waters had a history of treachery.

"The Coast Guard stays busy around here," he said. "An old colleague of mine tells a story about a catamaran that called mayday from the Farallones. The radio transmission said a wave had just come through the cabin, and that was the last anyone ever heard from them. Six people on board."

Mr. Cotter must have seen me turn white. We stood at the starboard railing, watching the bridge pass overhead. He put his hand on my shoulder.

"I'm sorry. I meant it as an interesting story, that's all. No need to worry. Captain O'Shay has made this trip a thousand times. But I'm afraid we're in for a little rough weather. The Farallones are notorious for choppy seas."

"How long will it take us?"

"Oh, four hours or so. Depends on the conditions. You can't really predict from here what it's going to be like out there. You know, it used to be an egging station. Gulls' eggs. A fellow named Robinson came out here in 1849 in search of eggs. Seems California didn't have many chickens, though I never heard why that was. Anyway, he and his brother brought back a boatload of murre eggs and sold them for a buck a dozen. I guess the eggs worked for baking, but they had red yolks, so people didn't much care for that. The brothers made three thousand dollars, which was an awful lot of money at that time. A couple of rival companies set up shop here when they heard about the Robinsons' success, and some enterprising gent designed egg shirts that the pickers could wear. The shirts held up to eighteen dozen eggs. A funny business. I think it ended in a shoot-out between the companies."

"Are there a lot of birds on the Farallones?"

"Oh, my," Mr. Cotter said. "More than you can dream. On the mainland, the eggers used to be known by the scars on their scalps from dive-bombing gulls. The birds are everywhere. You know, the Farallones were once known as the Devil's Teeth? Sailors named the islands that because they have a frightening outline against the sea. It's a foreboding place."

"Leave it to Tommy to pick a place like that for his wish."

"How's he doing, anyway?" Mr. Cotter asked, his eyes on the water.

"On the trip?"

"No, in general. With his health."

"It's not good," I said, watching a gull hover above our wake. "He can't put on any weight and he's prone to too many illnesses. He never complains, but you can see he has good days and bad days. He's spent years in the different doctors' offices. Sometimes he just seems tired of it all."

"Your mom gets some help with the medical costs?"

"Yes," I said. "She's only a hostess at a restaurant, so we get some help."

He nodded.

"I hope you don't think I'm prying," he said. "I just wanted to know the score a little bit so that I don't put my foot in my mouth. They can't release much information to volunteers like me at the foundation. Confidentiality of medical records and so on. Tommy's an awfully charming young man. I can't remember meeting anyone as forthright and all-around honest as he is."

"Everyone loves Tommy. He has no defenses. Everything has been stripped away and what's left is genuine."

"You're mature to see that," Mr. Cotter said. "A lot of teenagers wouldn't."

"You can't miss it with Tommy."

"Just the same, it's good to see a brother and sister who care for each other. He clearly thinks the moon sets on you."

"We're pretty close," I said.

I liked talking to Mr. Cotter. He asked me about school, but he wasn't like some adults who ask and then don't listen. He was old enough not to be rushed, or to think he had to be somewhere else. He offered his full attention. We talked a little more about New Hampshire, which seemed like a magical place in his memory.

While we talked, the seas grew rougher. Neither one of us said anything about it, but we both noted it and our conversation became laced with moments of silence when we listened to the waves. The *Gray Jay* began to labor more determinedly in the wallows, and the cresting waves grew to five or six feet. It didn't seem dangerous, but it didn't seem easy, either.

"I'm going to look for Tommy," I said after a while. "See how he's doing."

"He's up with the captain. I'll duck in and see how our group is faring. We have a thermos of hot chocolate if you're interested."

I climbed the short ladder to the captain's wheelhouse and pushed through the door. I knew at first glance that Tommy had a growing case of seasickness. His face looked white; when he smiled, it seemed to drain off his face, as if the muscles of his chin and cheeks couldn't sustain any co-ordinated movement. Captain O'Shay, on the other hand, looked entirely at home. He had a large elephant-ear cin-namon bun on the console in front of him, and he broke off pieces as he watched the horizon. He reminded me of the gulls that occasionally passed overhead. He was all belly and appetite.

"So this is the sister, is it?" he said when I stepped in-side. "Well, your brother here knows more about sharks than just about anybody who has taken this trip. Marine biologists included! We were just talking about elephant seals. That's the real stuff. When a white shark takes an elephant seal, you've never seen such blood."

"The blood is superoxygenated," Tommy explained. "Because elephant seals dive way, way down. They have to have more oxygen in their blood. More than other seals."

"And they're huge," Captain O'Shay said, eating more cinnamon bun. "Just enormous."

Then Captain O'Shay pointed with his right hand, the hand holding another wedge of cinnamon bun. I followed the line of his arm. A couple hundred yards away, a whale blew spray into the air. It looked like a teakettle coming to boil.

"We've got company!" Captain O'Shay said, then grabbed the microphone. He spoke into it, letting the group downstairs know he had spotted a whale. A gray whale, he thought, though he couldn't be sure from this distance. After he hung up the microphone, he explained that Mrs. Halpern's school had authorized a whale-watching trip. The sharks, he said, were just a sideline. Some people didn't think kids should be going out to watch a bloody shark attack, but personally he didn't agree. Nature was nature, and the sooner kids got used to it, the sooner their real education started.

That was when Tommy threw up.

He threw up without making it outside, or to a waste-basket, or to anything else that might have contained the mess. He threw up reflexively, and violently, and Captain O'Shay muttered, "Oh, crud," and I took off to grab towels. I hustled down the stairs, then ran into the cabin where the challenged kids sat sipping hot chocolate. I spotted Mom talking to Mrs. Halpern. I yanked a few hand towels off the table near the hot chocolate, then shot back up to the cabin. No one had moved. Tommy stood with his arms out at his sides, as if he couldn't believe what he had done, and Captain O'Shay stood on one leg to keep his feet free of vomit.

"It's okay," I said to Tommy.

He started to cry.

"It's okay," I said again, although I nearly gagged as I cleaned Tommy's chest and arms. I told him to step outside and if he needed to throw up, to do it over the rail.

"Port side," Captain O'Shay called after him as Tommy went out. "Not into the wind."

I bent and cleaned up the mess. I had to fight my gag response the entire time. Captain O'Shay moved his feet around to give me room to mop. It was disgusting. I bundled the towels together and stood when I finished.

"He's a good boy," Captain O'Shay said, looking

straight ahead. "He may not feel up to it in any case, but I doubt we'll be putting anybody over the side today. Too choppy. I think we'll just be sightseers."

"He wants to dive," I said. "It means everything to him."

Captain O'Shay nodded.

"Well," he said, "the sea has the final word. We'll check the conditions when we get there. Meanwhile, keep him in the fresh air and see how his belly reacts. If he can eat a little something, it might help him. Seasickness is a miserable state of affairs."

I carried the towels outside and found Tommy leaning on the railing. He had thrown up again, he said. He appeared white and shaky. I told him to take deep breaths. I told him to watch the whale. I told him he would feel better soon, though both of us knew that wasn't likely.

At first glance, I understood why the Farallon Islands had come to be known as the Devil's Teeth. They rose out of the ocean nearly vertically, their shores all rock, their outline black against the gray sea. The day had not grown any brighter, and the islands reminded me of a parody of a dark and stormy night: all mood and blackness and wind. Seals rested on every available rock, their bodies like gobs of mud on the islands' skin. Above it all the gulls and murres and terns floated like flies above a garbage can.

The *Gray Jay* moved within two hundred yards of the islands, but Captain O'Shay announced over the loudspeaker that the weather was rising. That meant, I
supposed, that we wouldn't stay long, and that the ride
home would be a humdinger. I didn't have to ask about
putting a diving cage over the side.

I'll give Mom this: she stood beside Tommy and shut up.
I know that sounds cruel, but it was the best thing to do.
She had fed him a little bagel and some peanut butter and
he appeared a bit steadier. The other kids had come on
deck, too, and Ms. Sprague hovered around them, press-
ing them together like dough. I imagined what she
thought: if a kid fell overboard and by some miracle didn't
drown, then you had to picture a shark swirling underneath the kid, and that was too painful to think about.
Now that her group had seen a whale—the real purpose of
their trip—I knew she would be just as happy turning
back. Mrs. Halpern, meanwhile, stood impassively by,
watching the islands and nibbling a bagel chip.

Over the loudspeaker, Captain O'Shay said he had contacted the research team that lived on one of the islands
and they had not experienced any attacks so far this morning. None of that quite made sense to me, and it was
only after Tommy explained that the Farallones had been
designated a national reserve, and that a team of marine

biologists lived there, studying the sharks and tagging them when possible, that I began to get a better idea of what Captain O'Shay meant.

I went to the other side of the boat and found Mr. Cotter standing at the railing, his eyes out to sea.

"How are you feeling, Bee?" he asked.

"Surprisingly, no problem."

"Some of the kids are getting sick," he said, lifting his chin to indicate the challenged kids behind him. "It's a long way to come to see a rocky set of islands."

"But the sharks are here," I said.

"That they are. I saw one feeding on an elephant seal out this way many years ago. It was before anyone gave this place much thought. Now, of course, the BBC did a documentary on it, and the government has put a research team out here. It's changed for the better. Anyway, one day I came here on a sailing trip with my son, and we had gone a little beyond this spot where we are now when we both saw a big commotion in the water. Neither one of us witnessed the attack, but we saw the shark close on the seal afterward. An elephant seal is an enormous animal, but the shark ate it in three or four bites. I remember the violence of the shaking most of all. The shark grabbed the carcass and shook it back and forth. Astonishing, really."

"Did it frighten you?"

"No more than bad weather would. You wouldn't want to come out here and do a slow breaststroke toward the island. The trick is to stay off the surface. That's why whites sometimes mistake surfboards for seals. They see a shape and little flipper hands coming off and they surge up from the bottom. The island research team has a shed full of old surfboards that have been bitten by whites. Daunting to look at, believe me."

"Do you think we'll see anything today?"

"We might. The weather won't bother them. The trouble is, we can't stay very long. It will get too rough for the kids."

"Tommy will be crushed if we don't see one."

Mr. Cotter nodded.

"You look after him, don't you?"

I shrugged.

"Taking care of someone can teach you a great deal," he said. "It's troublesome, and it's easy to get annoyed, but your heart, well, it gets stronger. You do it for Tommy, of course, but you do it for yourself, too. I took care of my wife at the end and I wouldn't trade that time."

"Was she sick for very long?"

"For quite a while. More than two years. I learned to love her in a different way."

"I understand," I said.

"I'm sure you do."

Right then Captain O'Shay came on the PA system and told us we had a kill.

TOMMY SHARK FACT #5: A great white does not chew its food. It rips off chunks of blubber and gristle and swallows them whole. A white has about three thousand teeth, triangular in shape and serrated along the edges. It uses the first two rows of teeth to grab and cut; the rows behind rotate in and take the place of worn-out or damaged teeth. After consuming a seal, a white may last a month or two before it needs to feed again.

• • •

Captain O'Shay leaned on the throttle pretty hard, and the boat lolled and banged through the waves on a wild ride. We headed away from the sun, that was all I knew, and circled around the islands. I ran upstairs to find Tommy. By the time I reached him, he had his head inside the captain's cabin, and had obviously engaged in a conversation and received a report. He pulled his head out a second later. He looked bright-eyed and happy.

"The Sisters," he said. "Mirounga Bay."

"The Sisters?"

Before he could explain, the boat jammed on a wave

and bucked, and Tommy nearly lost his balance. I grabbed him.

"Where's Mom?" I asked.

"She was sick. She went below."

I grabbed the back of his life jacket.

"Captain O'Shay said we want to be on the starboard side," Tommy said. "Let's go!"

We scuttled around the back of the boat, then cut across to the starboard side. I kept Tommy inside me, away from the railing. When we reached the starboard side, I spotted the islands again. They looked crueler from this angle, more horrible to think about. Birds churned everywhere. A plume of gulls circled like smoke from a pile of leaves.

"There!" Tommy pointed.

His voice went up. He nearly came out of his skin.

Blood. Bright red blood. Blood redder than any blood could be. Blood swirling away from a center, from a darkness in the water, from an ending you never want to think about. Blood like a flag widening on the sea as it traveled.

"Ten o'clock," Captain O'Shay said over the PA.

Tommy had spotted the kill faster than the captain. The boat rocked along, still several hundred yards away from the blood. Some of the challenged kids came out with Mrs. Halpern. She pointed her finger at the blood circle.

Whether the kids understood what she meant seemed impossible to say.

"Do you see anything?" I asked Tommy.

He shook his head.

"Just the blood," he said, his voice tight with anticipation.

"What did you mean, *the Sisters*?"

"The researchers call them the Sisterhood. About three or four females who hunt out here. They're deadly."

"I can't see the seal," I said.

"It's gone," Tommy said.

A second later we saw a fin. It passed so quickly it might have been a trick of our eyes. The fin went away from us and didn't slice the water for more than a heartbeat. Its tail flicked a little water behind it, then it disappeared.

"That was a shark, Tommy," I whispered. "A great white. You've seen a great white. You saw a kill."

He nodded. He reached over and took my hand. It took me a moment to realize he was having trouble breathing.

Late afternoon. Land breeze, the boat grinding closer to shore, gulls overhead. Seals running like black stitches through the surf. Tommy asleep with his head on my mom's lap, his feet on mine. A quiet moment. Empty Styrofoam cups of hot chocolate rolling in windshield-wiper half circles on the table. The challenged kids come in, go out, come in again. Mrs. Halpern sitting across the boat from us, a circle of knitting growing in her hands. A purse, she told my mother. A purse that would be washed ten times, shrunken, then felted and decorated. Tight, like boiled wool. Nothing, she promised, could fit through the weave. A gift for a grandchild, a girl, who lived in Palo Alto and went to Stanford and studied chemistry. Each stitch, she told my mother, is a thought.

Mr. Cotter drove us back to our hotel. He looked sleepy and windburned, but he tried to keep his voice high and animated for Tommy. Tommy sat up front. They talked about the Farallones and about the deep drop-off the islands created. Perfect shark ambush territory, Tommy said. Two strokes and the seals hovered over thirty feet or more of water. Dark rocks below. Plenty of cover for the great whites. A collision of two lives, but also a mutual benefit if you took the long view.

"What are your plans for tomorrow?" Mr. Cotter asked when we got closer to the hotel. He looked in the rearview mirror to meet my mother's eyes.

"We thought we'd have a lazy morning, then do some sightseeing," she said, her voice quiet and calm. "We have Monday, too. We fly out Monday night."

"I'm afraid I'm not going to be able to help out," Mr. Cotter said. "My team has a croquet match about a hundred miles south of here. I'll be gone all day. And Monday I'm booked."

"You've been very kind already," my mother said. "We didn't expect you to guide us, too."

"Well, at least we saw a shark," Mr. Cotter said, turning and smiling at Tommy. "Captain O'Shay said it looked like a juvenile. Maybe ten or eleven feet."

"You can measure from the fin to the tip of the tail," Tommy said. "Make a guess, anyway."

"He might have just been cleaning up," Mr. Cotter said. "Maybe a bigger girl took the seal to begin with."

"I couldn't believe the color of the blood," Mom said.

We had been over that. She said it to fill space.

We pulled up in front of the hotel a few minutes later. Mr. Cotter climbed out and came around to say goodbye. He hugged my mother, hugged me, then gave Tommy a handshake.

"I'm glad I met you," Mr. Cotter said to Tommy. "I'm sorry the weather didn't cooperate and allow us to put you in the cage."

"It's okay, Mr. Cotter. Thank you for taking me to see the islands."

"I've got your address," Mr. Cotter said. "If I make it back for a Dartmouth reunion, I'll look you up. Maybe we can take a hike."

Tommy nodded. Mr. Cotter suddenly had a kind, sad look in his eyes. He reached out and put his hand softly against

Tommy's cheek and ear. I realized, watching him, that he was a man with sons, a man whose heart would crack if anything happened to his boys. And here was Tommy.

"Okay," Mr. Cotter said, dropping his hand. "Good luck to you all."

No one can meet Tommy and remain unaffected. No one can help loving him. I saw it in Mr. Cotter's eyes. I've seen it a hundred times. Tommy is a light, a candle, whatever you want to call him. Sometimes he sheds light; sometimes he reflects it back at whoever looks at him. I don't even question it any longer. It just is. When I've read about saints in catechism classes, I've always thought they were probably people like Tommy. Not supernatural, not more godly than anyone else, but simple, quiet people whose humility was the most exceptional thing about them. Tommy never holds himself above others and never looks down on anyone. He meets people square. He believes in them, because he knows even in the dullest of us, or the most lame, a person resides there.

Mom's cell phone rang as I slid the key card into the hotel room door.

"Well, hi," she said when she fished her phone out of her purse, her voice turning instantly girlish, her eyes opening wide and glancing at me as if she had done something miraculous in receiving a phone call from a guy. "Jerrod, how nice to hear from you!"

Tommy groaned softly and shook his head. I slid the card out and handed it to her. She stayed in the hall. Tommy and I went inside. Even through the wall we heard her turn into Mom Barbie, her voice filled with curlicues.

"Hello, Jerrod," Tommy imitated her, his voice going up in a funny falsetto. "How do you do?"

"Good grief," I said. "You're almost as ridiculous as she is."

Tommy fell on the bed laughing. He picked up the TV remote and shot the set alive. He turned up the volume. He seemed tired and sleepy.

I told Tommy to change his clothes and then went to the bathroom and looked at my face. The wind had burned me as it had Mr. Cotter. I turned back and forth, trying to see how red I was. I had raccoon eyes from where my sunglasses had covered me. I pulled my hair into a ponytail and washed my hands, then I studied my face a little. I looked like certain kinds of terrier dogs, sharp and pointed, and way too serious. Before I finished, Mom knocked on the bathroom door and pushed through. She smiled. I knew what was coming.

"I'd like to meet Jerrod for a drink," she said. "That is, if you don't mind sitting with Tommy."

"And what if I do mind?" I asked, squeezing some moisturizer onto my hand. I rubbed it around my eyes and up on my forehead. It felt good on my skin.

"Do you really care or are you just giving me a hard time?" Mom asked, coming to stand beside me and inspecting herself in the mirror. She grabbed the moisturizer and smeared her face with it, too.

"Gee, I don't know, Mom, we're on a family trip and you want to go out on a date."

"For a drink, Bee," she said. "He's going to be nearby this evening and he just wants to meet for a drink. Sorry for trying to have a life."

"This is Tommy's trip," I said. "Four measly days."

"And we took him out and we saw a shark," Mom said, her eyes meeting mine in the mirror. "And last night we stayed together. Tonight I'd like to go out and meet a gentleman who said he wanted to buy me a drink. Is that a crime? I'll leave you money. You can go and get a pizza or whatever you like."

"Whatever," I said. "Knock yourself out, Mom."

"It's easy to be critical," Mom said, pushing her hand hard against her cheek to keep the flesh going up, not down, "but you try raising two children on your own."

"And that means you need to go out on a date?"

"It means," she said, emphasizing the *means*, "that on occasion I want adult company, yes."

"Adult male."

"It would be nice to have a man in my life, Bee. Sorry if that disappoints you."

"It's so predictable."

She looked at me.

"I won't be late," she said.

"Of course you won't."

"I'll always be your mother," she said, her voice crowding me somehow. "I'm afraid you're doomed."

"Lucky me. What's that supposed to mean?"

"Well, that none of us is perfect." She rubbed the last of the moisturizer away. "And that we're locked together, like it or not."

"That's got nothing to do with you going out on a date."

She shrugged. I shrugged back.

"She going?" Tommy asked from the bed.

I nodded.

He nodded.

"What do you want to eat?" he asked.

"I don't care. Want to get room service?"

"You think that's okay?"

"It's your trip, you little skunk boy."

"I've always wanted room service."

"Your wish is my command, master."

Tommy smiled. He was half asleep. We watched television.

The sun went down and I got up and closed the drapes. He pulled the bedspread over his chest but left his legs out. His chin almost rested on his chest. Mom came back and forth, dressing. The last time she went through the room she smelled of perfume.

After Mom left, Tommy ordered a turkey club with curly fries and a diet soda. I ordered a Philly cheesesteak with sweet potato fries. We watched an old episode of *Friends* while we waited for the food to arrive. The waiter who brought the food up was gray and creaky on his feet and had a gut the size of a backpack gummed onto his waist. His name tag said *Wayne.* He set the food down on the bench at the foot of the bed, then he hung around a little until it occurred to me that I was supposed to tip him. Luckily, I had seen Mom stash the envelope Mr. Cotter had given her for incidentals. I fished out five dollars and handed them to Wayne.

"Thank you, miss," he said.

"Thank you, Wayne," I said as if I had a choice.

I showed him out. Tommy tried to get up to get his food but he had a little trouble swinging himself out, so I carried it over to him. I spread a towel over his legs and put his plates on his lap. He needed to wear his vest soon, I knew. I grabbed my own food and sat next to him. We didn't talk much as we watched the cast of *Friends* act stupid. And when they did something that was supposed to be touching and the sound track made an *awwwww* sound, I looked at Tommy and crossed my eyes. I snagged some of his curly fries.

"You feeling okay?" I asked him when we were about halfway through our sandwiches.

"Just tired," he said.

"Try to eat. You had a long day."

"I'm not that hungry," he said.

I grabbed the remote control and turned the volume down. I put the back of my hand to his forehead, testing him for fever. His eyes looked glassy.

"We need to put you in the vest," I said. "Are you okay? What's wrong?"

He shrugged.

"Come on," I said. "Spill it."

He started to cry a little. He never does that.

"You didn't like today very much," I said. "Is that it?"

He wiped the back of his hand against his eyes. I got up and lifted the plates from his lap. He looked beat suddenly, and more defeated than I had ever seen him.

"You can tell me," I said. "Go ahead."

"It's nothing," he said around his tears. "It's just . . ."

"You're disappointed."

"I just thought it would be different. I thought I was going to dive in the cage. That's what they said. That was the whole point of coming out here. But it didn't happen."

"You saw a shark," I said. "And blood."

"Anyone could do that."

"I'm sorry. I get what you're saying."

"It's not your fault."

"I know. But I understand what you mean. It was nearly what you wanted, but it wasn't, and now you have to pretend that it was, right?"

He nodded.

"Remember the dress Mom bought me for the ninth-grade dance?" I asked. "I'd seen one that was exactly what I wanted, but then Mom went out and bought me something sort of like it and I had to pretend that it was perfect. Only it wasn't. And I went to the dance and I didn't feel pretty, and I hated the dress, hated everything about that night. So I don't blame you."

I put his vest on him and we sat for a long time watching television. By eight o'clock Tommy had fallen asleep with his arms out, the chest vibrations still jiggling his cheeks.

I waited up until midnight. Mom didn't come back.

SUNDAY

"You think she stayed over with him?" Tommy asked.

It was early morning. Tommy lay in bed, the remote in his hand. A single stream of weak light pushed through the crack in the curtains. I didn't say anything. Instead I rolled over and pretended to sleep. I listened to him flicking around the TV stations. He wasn't allowed to watch so much television at home and we didn't have cable anyway. He was being a little TV piglet.

He went to the cartoon station and stayed there awhile. The next time I looked up he had found some ridiculous show about guys going out in boats to catch Alaskan king crabs. The show consisted of big waves crashing over a small boat and the guys yelling back and forth to see if they were okay. Then Tommy went back to the cartoons.

"Why does she do that, Bee?" Tommy asked a little later.

"Ask her," I said, my face turned down into the pillow. "That's her stuff."

"Is she a sex fiend?" he asked.

I had to laugh.

"No, you little twerp," I said, lifting my head from the pillow, "your mother is not a sex fiend."

"Then why would she stay over there?" he asked, his eyes on the television. "She usually comes home no matter what."

"Not always." I sighed. "You should ask her."

"I'm asking you, Bee."

I sat up and pushed the hair off my face. My mouth tasted gross from the french fries. My lips still had salt on them.

"I think she's afraid of getting old," I said. "Afraid of ending up alone. It's complicated."

"But we're here," he said. "We're her family."

I nodded. I saw myself in the mirror behind the television and pushed my hair off my face more.

"She doesn't do it to be mean to us," I said. "She does it to make herself feel better. It's weird, I know. When she has a guy tell her she's cool and sexy and all that, then she feels better about herself. She isn't really thinking, she reacts to the moment."

"It's bogus," he said. "Really bogus."

"I agree."

"Is it a girl thing?"

"A little bit. But boys do it, too. Some boys go from woman to woman thinking anything that goes wrong is the woman's fault. They keep picking up the same rock and getting mad at it when it isn't gold."

"Did you just make that up?"

"Which part?"

"The gold thing. That's ridiculous."

"Is that so?" I said, then chucked my pillow at him. "Well, maybe it is."

I went into the bathroom and washed my face and brushed my teeth. When I returned, Tommy had the paper cup of soda on his belly from the night before. His straw poked around in the melted ice. He made a long sucking sound. I passed by his bed and looked out the window. Another good day weatherwise.

"Let's go get breakfast," I said. "Let's get out of this room. It's too nice out to stay cooped up."

"Let's go see Ty Barry," Tommy said, the straw making a little trombone sound on the plastic lid cover. "He doesn't live far from here."

"You can't just barge in on him."

"He knows we're around. He told me to call back today and let him know what our plans are. Not everyone is as uptight as you, Bee's Knees."

"You little punk," I said. "I should rough you up."

Another kid would have jumped to his feet and wanted to rumble, but it took Tommy three separate movements. Cup down. Slowly climb onto the bed. Assume a karate position.

"I could crush you," I said, taking a karate stance back at him.

"Hands of death," he said, waving his hands around.

"Beware the great white shark," I said, snapping my teeth and moving my hands to my forehead to form a fin. Then I moved slowly toward him like a shark cleaving water.

"Some puny shark, Bee's Knees," Tommy said, slapping my fin.

"You're too bony to eat, little boy. I want a big fat seal."

"Then you have to eat yourself, because you're the biggest, fattest seal around."

I pretended to bite his leg. He jumped from his bed to the

other bed and almost fell. When he regained his balance, he looked at me, his hands still up in a karate posture.

"Let's go before she gets back," he said. "Let's just go."

"You mean split? That wouldn't be very nice."

"She wasn't very nice to take off on us."

"She'll be really, really angry."

"Maybe that'll teach her a lesson."

"What lesson?"

"That you can't be a jerk and then expect people not to be jerky back at you."

"Is that one of the Ten Commandments or something?"

He dropped his hands.

"I want to go see Ty Barry," he said. "This is my trip. I'm going with or without you, Bee."

So we went.

FROM GOOGLE: Half Moon Bay is 25 miles south of San Francisco along State Route 1, the Cabrillo Highway, at 37°27'32"N 122°26'13"W37.45889°N 122.43694°W.

It is 10 miles west of San Mateo, 45 miles north of Santa Cruz. The 2000 census counted 11,842 people in the town, and 4,004 households.

We went looking for one person.
Ty Barry.

● ● ●

Dear Mom,

We'll be back in a day. We went to visit Ty Barry, a friend of Tommy's who lives out here. We'll call to let you know where we are when we get there. We took half of the money. We're not trying to be hurtful. We just got tired of waiting around, and seeing Ty means an awful lot to Tommy.

Love,
Bee and Tommy

I left the note taped to the bathroom mirror.

The second bus we caught out of San Francisco smelled of diesel and brake fluid. The driver, a guy named Oti, passed his eyes in a triangle from one mirror to the next. Rear, left side, right side. Then straight forward. He did it over and over again at the same pace. Now and then our eyes clicked when he checked the rearview mirror. He had half-closed eyelids and a half-filled-in mustache. Everything about him seemed to be waiting for something to arrive. I wanted to ask him about Half Moon Bay, but a sign on the pole above his seat said not to talk to the driver.

Tommy had been smart enough to take a seat on the west side of the bus, the side looking toward the ocean. Now and then we had a glimpse of something like ocean, or sand, or just greater spreads of light. It was Sunday morning and the bus ride felt lazy and empty.

"What are you doing down this way?" Oti asked us when we had ridden for about fifteen minutes. Only two kids had joined us on the bus and they sat far in the back, probably so that they could smoke.

"We want to see Mavericks," I said.

Oti's eyes darted around, then sought mine again.

"Mavericks?" he asked.

"A surf place," Tommy said. "They get monster waves that come all the way from the Aleutian Islands in Alaska. They have fifty-foot faces, some of them."

Oti shook his head to say he didn't know.

"I never heard of anything like that around here," Oti said. "But there's a lot of surfing going on."

"They get some shark attacks down this way, too," Tommy said. "It's in the bloody triangle."

"Oh, I know about those," Oti said, braking to let a car turn left in front of him. "Great whites, right?"

"Yes," Tommy said.

"Heck, I watch Shark Week every year on television.

Wouldn't miss it. You ever hear about kids fighting sharks in cages?" Oti asked, giving the bus gas.

"In Mexico?" Tommy asked.

"No, in Hawaii, where I'm from. Test of manhood. They found archaeological remains of cages," Oti said, stringing out the word *cageeessssss* until it sounded like something lethal, something like *alligatorsss*. "They put twelve-year-old boys down there with a spear, and the boys had to hold their breath and fight the sharks. Pretty awesome."

"Never heard of that," Tommy said.

"I'm telling you," Oti said. "Pretty wild stuff."

Tommy nodded. He had pushed forward on his seat so that he could see Oti better.

"Test of manhood, like sending African kids out to kill a lion. I'm not joking," Oti said, tapping the brakes a couple of times to let traffic swirl clear of him.

I smelled cigarettes from the back of the bus.

"Hey," Oti yelled into the front mirror, his eyes looking down the aisle. "You cannot be smoking in here."

The kids laughed.

"If I have to pull over," Oti said, "you won't be laughing."

Maybe the kids put the cigarettes out. It was hard to tell.

"A guy down here at Mavericks," Tommy said, his breath missing a little and pulling in his chest, "a shark rammed him from underneath. He was off to the side at a place called Mushroom Rocks, off by some deepwater kelp beds, just talking to a friend. The shark came up and knocked him into the air, and when he came down he had his arm over the snout of a great white. You imagine that? The shark took off like crazy with the guy riding him like you'd try to bulldog a steer, only a steer with teeth."

Oti shook his head and said, "Sweet cream of wheat."

"That was in 2000. The first attack ever at Mavericks," Tommy went on. "They've had one other that we know about."

"They mistake those surfers for seals, right?" Oti said, catching my eye in the mirror. "What's the matter? Your sister doesn't like sharks?"

He smiled at me. He was kind of cute in a way.

"How much longer?" I asked.

"Not far," Oti said. "You know where you want to get off?"

"I guess near the center of town," I said.

He nodded.

"I see the cigarettes, you dubbers," Oti shouted suddenly at the kids in the back. "Do you think I'm blind?"

Tommy ordered waffles and bacon and a tall glass of grapefruit juice. I ordered scrambled eggs, home fries, and wheat toast. A waitress brought the food in stages, almost as though she had to make a decision about each plate before it could join its buddies. She was in her twenties and had a vine tattooed across her neck and right shoulder. Under his breath, Tommy called her Poison Ivy, one of Batman's archenemies.

The restaurant was nice, though. It looked out on the water. It had taken us forty-five minutes to find a decent place after stepping off the bus. Oti had pointed us in the right direction to find the shopping center. He also told us the Ritz-Carlton, a gigantic resort on a hill overlooking Half Moon Bay, stood three miles from the beach. He found an old brochure on the dash of his bus. The brochure advertised horse trails and kayak rentals and a "two luxuries at once" deal where guests could rent a Mercedes for the day for sightseeing.

"It's hard to believe this is the place," Tommy said after Poison Ivy left the food. "I mean, it's so nice here, it's hard to believe that sharks are out there hitting people off surfboards."

"Only a few people," I said.

"They get kayakers, too, you know," he said, cutting into his waffle. "One of them lifted the nose of a kayak right out of the water and shook the boat until the guy fell out."

"You're nuts, you know that?"

Tommy wiggled his eyebrows at me.

"I think Oti liked you," he said. "He was checking you out."

"He was at my mercy," I said.

Tommy stopped sawing at his waffle.

"You're really pretty, Bee," he said, looking up at me. "A lot of guys think so."

"I know. They break down my door every weekend."

"You *are*," Tommy said, his voice surprisingly emphatic, his fork straight up from his plate. "You don't know it, but you are. And you'd have a boyfriend if you wanted one."

"Like who?"

"Like Ricky. And Jeff. Both those guys think you're smoking." Ricky and Jeff worked on the school paper with me and had come over to our place a few times. "I've heard them talking."

"Eat your waffles, you weirdo."

"You could date them no problem."

"Jeff is a nerd and Ricky is too self-involved. Besides, I don't have time for boys right now."

"Oh, I forgot, you don't have time for fun. You have to run the universe."

"You little bratasaurus."

"You need to chill sometimes, Bee."

"I'm not good at relaxing."

"You can say that again."

"Am I that bossy?"

"No," Tommy said, appearing thoughtful, "you just care

too much about things. You have to loosen up. You don't have to be the president of everything you join."

"It's always weird around boys, anyway. Half the time they just want to kind of tackle you and the other half they want to avoid you."

"Lots of guys are going to want to date you, Bee. Mom says so. She says you're becoming a swan."

"She's out of her mind. I'm no swan."

"Yes you are," Tommy said. "Mom says you're going to be drop-dead beautiful by the time you finish growing and she's right. You're the only one who doesn't see it."

"You both need glasses."

He looked at me. I knew the meaning of his look. Tommy didn't lie and he wasn't lying now. That was what he meant.

"Can you ask Poison Ivy for some honey?" he asked.

I got honey for him. Then we ate without talking. I was hungrier than I realized. We ate and looked out at the water and the entire morning had a good beach feeling about it. Tommy looked happy and healthy, and for the first time it felt like we had actually escaped on vacation. I thought about my mom and how angry she was going to be, but I didn't care. Tommy didn't care, either, which somehow made it okay that we had taken off on her. She had done the same to us. And I knew if we had stayed, she would have showed up midmorning with some lame excuse about a car not starting or losing track of time. Living with her was like missing a plane every day. I figured I would call her later.

"So," I said when we had made it through breakfast, "do you have Ty Barry's address?"

"Twenty-three Oakmont."

"You think he's really expecting us?"

"I called him from the hotel when you were showering. I woke him up." Tommy looked sheepish. "He wasn't mad. Just gave me the address and said to come down. Guys are a lot more laid-back about making plans."

"Oh, is that so?" I had to ask.

"Yes, Bee."

"You are so righteous," I said.

Tommy pretended to sip through his straw until his eyes crossed.

"We need to find a room," I said when he finished. "And you need to use the vest."

"I'm feeling good," Tommy said.

"Let's do the vest near the water, then we can track down Ty Barry's address," I said. "How's that for a plan?"

"Awesome," Tommy said, trying to be hip in his corny way.

He looked small and flushed in his booth.

"You are so square," I told him. "You're pitiful square. You're as square as a Ping-Pong table."

"Ping-Pong tables are rectangles," he said.

"You're as square as a square."

"Let's roll," he said. "Can you ask Poison Ivy for the check?"

I did. I left a decent tip. I counted the money in the envelope. We still had more than three hundred dollars, plenty for a room for a night.

"Oti thought you were a babe," Tommy teased me on the way out. "A New Hampshire hottie."

"You are so weird," I said.

But Tommy had already pushed out the door, and seagulls had already begun to cry.

TOMMY SHARK FACT #6: The great white shark reproduces only every two to three years and has litters of about five to ten pups. Great white sharks can be found in all coastal temperate waters, whether three feet or 1,280 meters deep. They are found on the coastlines that stretch from California to Alaska, the East Coast of the USA, most of the Gulf Coast, Hawaii, most of South America, Australia (except the north coast), New Zealand, the Mediterranean Sea, West Africa to Scandinavia, Japan, and the eastern coastline of China to Russia. A great white shark has five gill slits.

Great whites have made a return to Cape Cod and other Eastern beaches. They never left, really, but with better ecological standards, seals have also managed a return. Wherever seals live, white sharks follow. In 2009, a group of tourists on a fishing boat watched in amazement as a great white ambushed a sea lion about seventy yards off a crowded Cape Cod beach. With more people in the water all the time, and the fitness athletes swimming greater distances in the ocean, shark-human collisions are unavoidable.

● ● ●

Shade of a palm. Tommy sitting with his arms away from his body, the vest vibrating. Gulls slicing back and forth, sometimes landing at our feet to ask for handouts. Half Moon Bay rolling in, rolling out. A half mile out, waves break, become white, then green, then roll and collect themselves until they swell and fall again in the bay. *Mavericks*, Tommy has said. Home of the GWS. Home of the kelp beds where sea otters rest on their backs and crack abalone against their chests. The great whites pass through the kelp like gangsters coming through a beaded curtain. Tommy's eyes stayed focused on the water, his lips jiggling a little with the vibration; his imagination, I knew, trained on the water, on the deep black floor of the sea where the whites patrol. Seal and shark. He says the ocean is not quiet underneath the waves. He listens to the sound of the ocean on his computer. Crackling and popping, the flip-flop of water and waves and things swimming for their lives. The cleave of the shark's fin, the sound of sand poured on paper, the water parting and returning around it, the gelatinous eyeball covered by a translucent membrane as it bites.

"You okay?" I asked, as much to get out of my own thoughts as to determine his status.

He nodded.

"A little longer," I said.

He nodded again.

We took a cab to Ty Barry's house. Tommy said we would know it because it was painted pink. I saw it before the driver slowed the cab. A pink, flat house. A lawn that had given up hope and had returned to sand. A tricycle on the sidewalk leading up to the house and three tubs of plants, some sort of succulents, that had died and turned yellow. The pink paint had peeled from the wall closest to the ocean, and underneath the paint the wood had turned silver. Three red Frisbees rested on the asphalt roof like hatches or spectacles. Music blasted from the backyard, or from inside the house—it was impossible to tell.

Tommy squeezed my hand before we climbed out.

"It'll be okay," I said, knowing he gets nervous around new people.

"I don't look like anybody," he said.

"What do you mean, Tommy?"

He shrugged. He had his head down.

"What is it?" I whispered.

"I probably don't look like someone Ty Barry would want to be friends with."

"Oh, Tommy. You have to trust people. He'd be lucky to know you."

"He's done a lot . . . you know, been places and done things, and I'm just E.T."

"Tommy, you have a heart like a lion. You're the kindest person I've ever met."

He shrugged again. Then he nodded. I paid the driver and we got out. For a second before we went up the walk, I saw Tommy not as my brother, but as a small boy, sick for life, his head too big, his body too weak, his soul open to everyone. His expression rested between hope and fear, as though he knew better than to expect too much but couldn't help himself. I felt my heart clump and had to look away. When I looked back, he had started up the walk, his little backpack bobbing against his spine.

"Tommy," I said and he turned around.

"What, Bee?"

"You're a great kid, Tommy. I want you to know that."

And where most kids would shrug, or make a face, Tommy did what he always does. He walked over to me and hugged me. My brother, Tommy.

"It sounds like they're around back," Tommy said after we had knocked on the front door a couple of times and got no answer. His face looked worried.

"Let's go around, then," I said.

He paused. I took him by the hand and led him a few steps. After that, I dropped his hand and followed him. The music got louder as we circled around. A large gray stockade fence walled off the backyard. Tommy pushed open the gate. Music crashed out at us and we saw people collected in the early-afternoon light. The backyard appeared bright and dry, and it took me a second to notice that someone had built a wooden half-pipe as long as the house. An old picnic table stood next to a small patio that led into the kitchen. Two teenage boys sat on the picnic table watching a third roll down the slope of the half-pipe. The boy on the half-pipe wore a helmet.

The boys on the table looked up when we stepped through the gate. The skateboarder rolled back and forth, the wheels changing pitch depending on how fast he shot down the sides.

"Does Ty Barry live here?" Tommy asked, but the boys

squinted and tightened their faces to say they hadn't heard him.

"Ty Barry?" I called, loud enough for them to hear over the music.

Before they could answer, another guy, older than the three with skateboards but still in his twenties, stepped out of the kitchen. He was tall and lean and tan and barefooted. He had long wavy hair clipped back in a ponytail. He couldn't have been more of a surfer-dude type. A tattoo of a sailing ship covered part of his upper arm and shoulder.

"Ty?" Tommy asked.

"You got me," Ty Barry said. "And you must be Tommy from New Hampshire."

Ty walked over and held out his hand. He and Tommy did a sort of abbreviated soul-shake that surprised me because I didn't know Tommy had ever tried one before. I shook hands afterward. Ty smiled. He had white, white teeth and smooth skin.

"Let me turn down the music," Ty shouted so that we could hear. "That's my brother, Little Brew, on the halfpipe. He's sixteen."

Ty waved at the three boys, signaling that he was cutting the music. Then he trotted into the kitchen and a second later the music went down to a realistic level. Little Brew jumped off his board and let it roll up the slope without him. When he pulled off his helmet, my stomach did a small roll. He was jaw-droppingly handsome, with brown eyes and hair down past his ears. He had perfect shoulders, wide and muscled, and his forearms moved when he motioned with his hands. If he knew he was amazingly gorgeous, he didn't act it. He smiled. He couldn't have bought a better smile. It was natural and friendly. The sun had turned his hair dirty blond and his skin was the color of apple butter. For a second I stared at him, not quite believing that such a boy existed outside of movies. I couldn't move.

"You the guys from New Hampshire?" he asked, coming over to shake hands. "The sharkies?"

He did the soul-shake thing with Tommy. They finished with a minor chest bump. Then he nodded at me.

"I'm just along for the ride," I said, my throat tight. "I'm Tommy's sister, Bee."

Little Brew looked at me for the longest time. I didn't know what else to say, if anything. Tommy saved me.

"I study great whites," Tommy said, looking first at me, then at Little Brew. "Just as an amateur."

"Well, dudes," Little Brew said, "say hello to my peeps. This is Frankie and Kobie."

We shook hands. Frankie and Kobie both had boards and Kobie climbed up to start his own routine. He did some tricks that I recognized from films I'd seen on MTV, but I didn't know what they were called. He zipped back and forth, nearly reaching the top on some moves and hanging there as though he wanted to use the board to plane the edges of the ramp. I didn't dare look sideways at Little Brew for fear of doing something obviously dorky.

"You like boarding?" Little Brew asked finally. "You guys can sit down, you know? Sit here and watch."

"Thanks," Tommy said.

We moved over to the picnic table, and I helped Tommy off with his backpack. Meanwhile Ty Barry returned from inside carrying a surfboard. Tommy stood up as soon as he saw it. He *knew*. When Ty slid the board onto the table, Tommy nodded.

A perfect circle of teeth marks covered the midsection.

"Unbelievable," Tommy said.

He reached out his hand and touched the teeth marks. The fiberglass board appeared slightly sprung with the impact from underneath. The teeth marks closed over the widest section, and it didn't take much imagination to see how an arm dangling over or a hand cupping water in mid-paddle would have been cut free as simply as a carrot.

"I've seen pictures," Tommy said, awestruck, his hand going back and forth over the board, "but it's way different seeing it in person."

"Everyone says that," Ty said, obviously a veteran at

going through this. "It's always amazing to get people's re-actions. Some people can't take their eyes off it."

"Do you mind saying what it was like?" Tommy said.

"Oh, here he goes again," Little Brew said, and Frankie shook his head and jumped onto the half-pipe to get away. "He's told this story a million times. With every new shark attack, he gets calls from reporters and it all starts up again."

"It was loud," Ty said, ignoring his little brother. "I mean, it was such a weird sound to hear in the middle of the ocean, this loud crushing sound of its teeth going into the board. I e-mailed you most of this stuff, though. You know the details."

"Yeah, but it's like seeing the board," Tommy said. "I want to hear you say the words. Did you feel like the water was sharky? Before it happened, I mean."

"It felt like it does before a storm. Quiet and calm, but the type where you sense that something big is coming. A guy I know says that a great white makes everything around it quiet. Fish scatter and seals take off. It's like the best gun-slinger in the world stepping into an old western bar."

"You should take them up to the cove," Little Brew said, his eyes touching mine for a second. "To show them the sea lion."

"A sea lion washed up with a giant bite out of its neck yesterday. Great white, most likely. The seal probably got away, but it bled out and then washed up."

"It happens," Little Brew said. "But the lifeguards may haul it off, so if you want to see it, you should do it sooner rather than later."

"You still surf?" I asked Ty.

"Sure," he said. "I figure the chances of a guy getting attacked twice by a shark are out of this world, so I'm the safest guy in the water."

"The sets are up to about twenty feet," Little Brew said. "They're building. You can come out with us tomorrow if you like. It's Columbus Day. No school."

"We wouldn't miss it," Tommy said before I could object. "Right, Bee?"

"Well, we'll see," I said. "We have to catch a plane tomorrow night."

"First thing in the morning," Little Brew said. "A whole crew is going out. There may even be some people filming for a promo. The big wave contest is in November."

I looked at Ty. He looked at me. And he nodded.

It was the kind of nod that said he would take care of Tommy.

I nodded back, our eyes making sure.

We drove a beat-up conversion van to see the dead seal in the afternoon. Little Brew sat in back with me, his body splayed out, his bleached shorts ripped here and there. He wore a red bandana around his head and I saw the tattoo of a nautilus shell on his right calf. Tommy rode shotgun and Ty drove. We kept the windows down. It felt good to be driving next to the ocean, the breeze filled with salt. I wasn't sure what Ty had told his brother, but both of them treated Tommy with care. They didn't baby him, exactly. They teased him gently, telling him he was out of control about sharks. Little Brew said Tommy needed a Native American name to protect him from the sharks, so he played around with ideas until he came up with Snow Pony. It was such a goofy name that it worked, and I watched Tommy swell each time they used it on him, jazzing him up and telling him he was way too East Coast. No one had ever given him a nickname before. No one had ever included him so easily.

We stopped at a convenience store and bought ten Arnold Palmers, a half lemonade, half ice tea drink that Ty and Little Brew drank like water. Tommy took a few sips of one, then passed it to me. It tasted sweet and a little tart.

"So what's Little Brew mean, anyway?" I asked when we got underway again. "Is that your Native American name?"

"Oh, man," Little Brew said. "You don't even want to know."

"Tell them," Ty said, his eyes looking in the rearview mirror. "Or I will."

Little Brew sighed and said, "There was a baseball player a long time ago named Harmon Killebrew. He was my dad's favorite player, because my dad was from Minnesota and Harmon Killebrew was like the only decent player to ever play for the Minnesota Twins in those years. So somehow I got it into my head that his name was Little Brew and they didn't correct me or anything for about, I don't know, a hundred years. They thought it was cute every time I said it, and of course I was being a donkey."

"My dad would make an announcer's voice and say, *Now batting, Jasonnnnnn Little Brew,*" Ty said. "And my dork little brother used to think it was the right name."

"It stuck," Little Brew said. "That's how it goes."

"So your real name is Jason?" I asked.

He nodded.

"Little Brew is way better," I said.

He smiled. His leg slid over a little and brushed against my calf. I felt a stone roll off a big pile in my gut. It kept going down the stones below it and rattling like an avalanche. I was afraid if he spoke I wouldn't be able to hear him.

"You think so?" he asked. "I went through this thing last year where I started asking people to call me Jason. Teachers and friends. But no one stuck to it. Some people say L.B. But no one calls me Jason."

"How long have you been surfing?" I asked him.

"I started surfing way young. They just put a board in the shallow water and let me jump on and off it. I was, like, three or something. Then you start climbing up on it and riding a little. Ty learned the same way. Our dad got us into it."

"You know, my dad had a white trail him once," Ty said, looking over at Tommy and changing the subject. "He was in a kayak with a group of people and the white trailed behind him for about fifty yards, then disappeared. A big fin, my dad said."

"We have some weird shark mojo in this family," Little Brew said. "No doubt about it."

"Do your parents live at the house?" I asked.

"Divorced, like, to the tenth degree," Little Brew said. "Mom's down in Mexico doing art tiles and Dad sells surgical supplies. He travels a lot. They bought our place as kind of a beach house years ago, but we took it over. Dad comes whenever he can."

"Snow Pony," Ty said, pulling into a parking lot next to some dunes with a path running down the center, "you ready to see some shark damage?"

"Bring it on," Tommy said.

I had to help him climb down out of the van. Tommy didn't like that, but he endured it. While the guys were still on the other side of the van, Tommy leaned close to me.

"Little Brew is *so* into you," he whispered.

"Cut it out, you weirdo," I whispered back.

"I know what I know." He held up his two fingers like

bull's horns, jabbing at me to make his point. He was feeling good and I couldn't help smiling. I also couldn't help thinking about what he said.

"I hope they haven't moved it," Little Brew said, coming around the backside of the van. "Frankie saw it here yesterday."

We smelled it before we saw it. Seagulls flocked the air above it and even a few crows hopped on the dunes, looking down like old ministers waiting their chance. We had to go over a small rise and I stopped to help Tommy kick out of his shoes. Ty and Little Brew were already barefooted. I stepped out of my flip-flops and the sand came up cool and smooth between my toes. Even with the horrid smell, the ocean air pushed around and filled in any empty places not given over to the dead-animal odor.

We came to a golden retriever before we came to the seal. A man dressed in a fleece and baggy shorts walked toward us, his face red. He didn't look happy. I understood why a moment later when I smelled the dog.

"Dead seal down there," the man said, then pointed to the dog. "This bonehead rolled in it."

"He reeks, dude," Little Brew said, stepping sideways to let the dog pass. "Why don't you let him swim?"

"I did," the man said, and yanked the dog after him.

"Seal guts get kind of ripe," Ty said.

"You imagine that dog in the car with you?" Little Brew said.

Then Tommy saw the seal. He walked toward it as fast as he had the night at Fisherman's Wharf, his eyes straight ahead, his gait cut by a limp. The gulls lifted at his approach. He waved his hand as if to dismiss them, as if to say he would take over now. They scattered and banked in sideward glides.

Even in the sand, even after the gulls had been at it, and the crows, I still saw the violence of what had occurred. So did Tommy. The blood along the seal's neck shone dull and cruddy like a rusted pipe. The knuckles of muscle and veins, the cords of tendons and strings of flesh, looked bruised and shortened by the savage bite. Somehow the tide had delivered the seal well onto the beach, and the waves that floated forward and back beyond the body seemed incapable of retrieving it.

It stunk. It stunk so hard it filled my nose and made me turn away, but Tommy went forward and knelt beside it. He grabbed a nearby stick and prodded at the neck. Whatever the seal had been, whatever its power to face the waves and the dark sharks flying up at it from below, had passed into the sand, had evaporated like air from a balloon. Death had flattened the sleek body.

It made me sick to go near it. I felt like retching. To my relief, Ty walked over and knelt beside Tommy. I stood next to Little Brew.

"They decapitate them a lot," Tommy said, still examining the seal with the stick. "Doesn't look like a gigantic white did it, but you can see it was a bite."

"It's not uncommon to have them wash up," Ty said. "This time of year, the whites are hunting here."

"You'd think with a bite like that, he'd never be able to get away."

"Yeah, it's nasty. But could be the shark was distracted. Could have hit a juicier one, maybe. You never know."

"You guys are ghouls. You're a little weird about this stuff," Little Brew said, and smiled at me. "Bee and I are going for a swim. You want to go for a swim?"

I wondered if it occurred to him that he was inviting me to go swimming where a shark had killed a seal a day or two before. I shook off any dread, glad that I had changed into my swimsuit back at the house.

"Sure," I said. "First swim in the Pacific."

"We're coming," Ty said. "Have you seen enough, Snow Pony?"

"I just never knew it was like this exactly," Tommy said, his eyes still on the bite mark. "It's awesome."

"They got to get them dead before they can eat them," Ty

said. "They really hit hard. The first bite probably kills most seals. It's a big impact."

"I can't believe you were hit like that," Tommy said.

"If it hadn't hit the board, I would've been a goner," Ty said. "You can see how it goes when you look at that seal."

Ty stood and dusted his knees free of sand. Tommy followed. Their movement shook some flies away from the body. The flies shifted, lifted, then resettled.

We followed the path to the water's edge. The afternoon sun rode a half dozen hands higher than the horizon. Early evening, late afternoon. The ocean rolled at us and collapsed on the sand and shells, then pulled back again. Little Brew pulled off his shirt and ran into the ocean. He dove into the first wave and reappeared fifteen feet out beyond the breakers. Ty laughed. I surprised myself by swinging my backpack down, stripping out of my shirt and shorts, and trotting to the water's edge. Little Brew didn't shout or make a big deal out of being in the water and I liked that about him. I waded in, trying to be casual, and when I got to my waist I flexed forward and dove.

As corny as it sounds, I couldn't help thinking: I am swimming in the Pacific Ocean.

I checked off a little box in some sort of quirky Beatrice Winterson life list.

Little Brew swam over. He looked irresistible, his hair wet and hanging down, his skin shiny with water. He swam beautifully, moving through the waves with total ease. I treaded water beside him, too nervous to put my feet down on the sand.

"Chilly, huh?" he asked. "Is it cold in New Hampshire when you swim?"

"Freezing," I said. "We don't really swim. We just duck in and out."

"Do you have coastline?"

"Seventeen and three quarter miles," I said.

He looked at me funny, so I added, "They made us memorize our state facts in fifth grade. Purple finch, state bird. Purple lilac, state flower. Pumpkin, state vegetable. Tallest mountain, Mount Washington. That kind of stuff."

"Impressive."

"Dorky," I said.

"Impressively dorky."

We didn't say anything for a little while, then I thanked him for being so kind to Tommy. His face softened.

"Ty loves the kid, so it's no biggie," Little Brew said. "I mean it. He e-mails with Tommy all the time. That whole shark thing is too big to just forget about, but you can't keep talking about it forever, either. It helps Ty to sort it out with Tommy. They have a bond about it all."

"Well, it means the world to Tommy. A lot of kids his age aren't quite as accepting."

"He's a cool kid. Ty said he has cystic fibrosis. So it affects his lungs?"

"Yes," I said. "He has trouble breathing and keeping the passageways cleared."

"That's a tough break."

Little Brew swam closer. His handsomeness seemed almost radioactive, like it glowed from him. I'd never let myself really like a boy before, but no boy had ever captured my attention like Little Brew. We kept looking at each other, and sometimes it seemed like it was *that* look, and sometimes it didn't. And then I realized I didn't really know *that* look, but I felt myself wanting to melt into him. I wanted to soak into him and let my heart beat be his heart beat, his skin my skin. I had to force myself to breathe.

"He's lucky to have you for a sister," Little Brew said. "You're obviously crazy about the kid. A lot of sisters wouldn't be into hanging out with their little brothers."

"He's the best person I've ever met. And that's dorky to say, too."

Little Brew smiled.

"I like dorky. Besides, I'm close to Ty. He didn't have to let me live with him after our parents split up. He could have just gone off and done his thing, but he made sure I was okay. Ty is kind of a natural dad-type. My father isn't, but he is. Weird, I know."

"And your mom? What's she like?"

"She's arty. Into primitive art. She's kind of worried she's missing out on life if she isn't painting something or traveling somewhere. Kids weren't exactly her top priority."

"I have a mom like that."

He nodded. "Then you know how they get easily distracted."

Little Brew put his feet down on the bottom and the water came to his chin. He tilted his head back to keep his nose and mouth free. He held out his arm.

"Here, hold on," he said. "You can't tread water forever."

I reached over and took his forearm. He smiled. The water moved me up and down, back and forth. I brushed against him and I felt like my heart might beat so hard it would break through my ribs. This is not happening, I thought. But it was. The most irresistible boy I had ever seen was holding me up in the waves off a California beach.

"See?" Little Brew asked.

"It's great."

"And it's not cold, right?"

"No, it's perfect."

Then for one instant, for one wave, I thought he might kiss me. Our eyes locked. A wave brought my body against his, my chest against his, my arms against his, and just as quickly the wave moved us apart.

"We have to be careful with Tommy," I said, because I couldn't think of what else to say.

"Not one bit," Little Brew said, joking. "Go big or go home."

Waves kept coming, lifting us up and setting us down. Salt lined my lips. I wondered what my girlfriends back home would think of me swimming with Little Brew, the cutest boy any of us had ever seen. Finally he lifted his arm to let me go, then he swam away and dove down, staying under for a good stretch. When he came up, he twisted onto his back and floated. Like an otter, I couldn't help thinking. Aqua-boy.

By the time we came out of the water, Ty had a small bonfire going. He had dug a hole in the sand and then walked around the beach until he found some trash and twigs. Ty said it was an Indian fire. White men, he said, build a big fire and sit far away from it; Indians build small fires and sit close. What it mostly meant, I realized as I dried my hair beside it, is that he had only a little fuel. But the flames looked lovely in the afternoon light. Tommy sat next to the fire and leaned back on his backpack. I loved seeing him relaxed and being part of something for a change.

"We should call Frankie and Kobie and tell them to bring us some wood," Little Brew said. "And some tofu pups."

"You guys veggies?" Tommy asked.

"You laugh," Little Brew said, "but Ty here thinks the shark didn't take him because he's a vegan. He uses no animal products. I'm just a simple veg beside him."

"Wonder why the shark bit at you in the first place if it was picking up your vegan vibe," Tommy said, looking at Ty.

"Yo, Snow Pony," Ty said. "I didn't expect to be dogged by you."

"Speaking of phone calls," I said, and glanced at Tommy. "Could I borrow your cell for just a second to check in with my mom? We kind of ditched her this morning."

"No problem."

"Don't tell her where we are, Bee," Tommy said, his voice even and strong. "She'll just mess things up."

"I've got it," I said. "But she knows about Ty."

"She doesn't know where he lives," Tommy said. "And she's not a detective. She's not going to track us down."

"She could call the police."

"She's not going to call the police," Tommy said. "She's just going to be pissed, that's all."

Ty reached into his pocket and handed me his phone. I walked off about twenty yards, sat on the sand, and dialed Mom's cell number. She picked up on the first ring.

"Where the hell are you?" she said, separating each word as if she could bite it.

"South of San Francisco," I said. "We're fine, Mom."

"You are so grounded, Bee," she said, her voice bubbling with bile. "You are even more than that. This is incredibly disrespectful. This is the most disrespectful thing anyone has ever done to me."

"You left him, Mom."

"I went on a date!" she said, her voice zooming up in volume. "You have no idea at your age what it's like for a woman my age."

I didn't say anything.

"Put Tommy on the phone," she said.

"He's not next to me."

"I don't care where he is," she said. "Put him on the phone. Now."

"He's okay," I said. "He's having a good time."

"Bee, what in the world are you thinking? You're not thinking, are you? Your brother is very sick and you should know that by now. I want to talk to him."

"We'll be back tomorrow afternoon. Maybe evening."

"We have to fly out on the red-eye tomorrow, young lady. I saw you took the money, too."

"We took *some of* the money. We said so in the note," I told her. "It's Tommy's money."

"I have never in my life felt so angry."

"Sorry, Mom. We weren't trying to hurt you."

She blew up at that.

"Not trying to hurt me, huh?" she yelled. "This is the most passive-aggressive behavior I've ever seen. You do exactly what you like, you abandon me, and you say you had no intention of hurting me. You have the emotional IQ of a child, Bee."

"What about you, Mom? What about . . . Never mind."

I wanted to point out again that she had abandoned us, that she was the one who hadn't come home, but that would have been tossing gasoline on a fire. Mom flashed on things like that. Besides, she had a point. I probably *did* want to send her a message, passive or otherwise, and I didn't particularly care what she thought of it. But I held my tongue. Silence worked better than argument.

"All right," she said, trying to be calm, "tell me where you are and I'll come and get you."

"I'm not going to do that," I said. "I'm sorry, Mom. I really am."

"What did you just say?"

"I said we're spending the night here and then we'll be back to the hotel late tomorrow afternoon. We'll be there before the flight no matter what. We'll call when we're on our way."

"I won't stand for this, Bee. I will not be treated this way."

"I'm going to hang up now, Mom. I'm not trying to be mean."

"I've got your cell number. Are you at that surfer's house? The one hit by the shark, Ty something? I'll report you to the police."

"If that's really what you want to do, Mom, I can't stop you. But you will break Tommy's heart if you do that."

"I'm the one who has to look after his safety, Bee," she said. "I'm his mother."

"I know that."

I heard her breathing hard. Then she began to cry. I didn't blame her. I would have cried, too, in her position. I wanted to say something consoling, but anything I thought of seemed too condescending. For just a second, I considered telling her where we were, what we had planned, and asking her to join us. She would like the boys, I knew, but she wouldn't like the idea of putting Tommy in big surf. She wouldn't mean to do it, but she would undermine him, start talking about the danger involved, and little by little she would pry the whole idea out of his head. I couldn't risk it. Tommy deserved to have a day filled all the way to the top. Just one day. And with Mom around, it wouldn't happen.

I hung up softly. A few minutes passed and the phone rang. It was my mom's cell number and I switched the phone to Vibrate. I didn't answer it. I looked over instead at the campfire. Tommy had stood up and was doing some ridiculous gangster-type movements and the guys were laughing. Laughing hard. It wasn't phony laughter, or laughing just to please the cystic fibrosis kid, but genuine laughter from down in their bellies. They saw Tommy as I saw him. I started to shiver, and the phone kept buzzing in my hand.

TOMMY SHARK FACT #7: Probably the most famous shark-attack victim is a guy named Rodney Fox. The attack occurred in Australia, south of Adelaide, during a spear-fishing tournament off Aldinga Beach. Fox sustained bites on his arm and chest area. He fought back by sticking his fingers in the shark's eyes and cut his hand on the shark's mouth in the process; during a second attack, Fox managed to fend the shark off by grabbing the animal's snout. Running out of air, Fox tried to make it to the surface, but the shark bit a dead fish attached to Fox's belt. The shark dragged Fox across the sea bottom before finally releasing him.

The injuries Fox sustained were massive. The shark fractured all the ribs on Fox's left side, collapsed his lung, jabbed through his scapula, and uncovered his spleen. Fox nearly died from blood loss. Some experts say his wet suit saved him by keeping the organs in place. Doctors administered 462 stitches. Part of the great white's tooth is still embedded in Fox's wrist.

The coolest thing about Fox from Tommy's standpoint is that Fox became one of the world's leading defenders of great whites. Instead of going on a quest to kill sharks, Fox opened a great white dive business and serves as a consultant and speaker about sharks. He is an advocate for shark education and shark awareness, which is what Tommy believes in, too.

Fox went back in the water less than a half year later. Tommy says Fox is tougher than anyone.

● ● ●

We got to sleep around two in the morning. Tommy should have been exhausted, but the boys pumped him up and sassed him and he loved it. They even joked when he was on the chest massager, making him say words so that his voice was garbled and came out like the Terminator's. They made him recite "Mary Had a Little Lamb," then say *I'll be back,* then *Here's Johnny* from *The Shining*. I would have stopped them there, but then they made him suck in helium from a balloon a friend got at the mall, and Tommy had to say a bunch of lines from *Anchorman* while they all doubled over. Tommy was a star, at least for the time being, and when he said *I'll wear sex panther,* which was one of the lines from *Anchorman,* the boys could hardly control themselves.

I had to fight hard not to interfere, not to make everyone go easier on him. Guys kept piling into the house and then leaving, and a few girls swung by, too. The group could have gone another way, heading to the skate ramp or finding something else to do, but Ty and Little Brew kept Tommy in the center. Tommy started to nod off a few times, but they wouldn't let him. They threw pillows at him if he faded and eventually he got a second wind.

After everyone left, it was just the four of us sitting on two beat-up couches. Ty and Little Brew talked about what it was like to be out on a board in big waves, to feel the whole world lift and begin to carry you forward, knowing the wave had come all the way from the Aleutians in Alaska, that it had run a couple thousand miles just to throw its guts against the California shore. Nothing like it, they said. Nothing as sweet. They rode big boards—guns, they were called—and once you headed down a wave that size, fifty feet of water, the top just turning a little in a horse mane, and then the slow arch, the crack that came as you shot down the wave face and began to cut, it was beyond words. And when the waves caught you, as they inevitably did, then that was something, too, something weird and otherworldly, because you were dragged below, your board yanking at your hip socket, the bottom sometimes hitting you, trying to detain you, and part of you didn't know which way was up. But you held your breath and let the waves churn you. You couldn't fight. You had to give in, to face your fate, and except for every once in a great while, the board brought you up and you had no problem. Nowadays they had Jet Skis that shot in to help you, Jet Skis that could ride over the biggest waves, mostly, and pull you to safety, running parallel to the beach until you escaped the surf wash. Sometimes you just lay on your board afterward and coughed your ribs out; other times you felt ready to go again. And sometimes, though rarely, you realized you needed to quit for the day because the sea felt too hungry. You had to get out of there and head back to land.

Tommy had been listening intently. Then in a soft, late-night voice, he said that when the air wouldn't come into his lungs, he would imagine being able to breathe through his eyes, or to suck in air through his skin, the way he thought frogs could, which made him feel like an amphibian. Then none of us said anything. We sat and listened to the wind pick up outside, and finally Ty and Little Brew headed to bed. They slapped five with Snow Pony. And Tommy and I went to sleep feet to feet on the couch, Tommy's smelly socks carrying the whole day's heat with them, his breath ragged and heavy and never quite full.

MONDAY

COLUMBUS DAY

"Shhh," someone whispered. "Bee? You awake?"

I sat up. I didn't know where I was. Then I saw Little Brew bending over the couch. He had an armful of blankets. He wore a Windbreaker and an absurd pair of earmuffs. The band of the earmuffs held back his hair.

"Want to see some shooting stars?" he whispered.

"Where?" I asked, not quite awake.

"Just out in the back. We have an old tree house."

"What time is it?"

"Around three-thirty. It's Columbus Day."

I swung my legs off the couch. Little Brew handed me a

sweatshirt and a Windbreaker. The sweatshirt smelled like him. Then he grabbed my hand and led me through the dark living room. A light in the vent above the stove kept the kitchen dull and quiet. He took back the Windbreaker as I pulled the sweatshirt over my head. The sweatshirt said *Big Waves*. I told him to wait a second, then I ducked into the bathroom off the kitchen and washed my face. I squeezed soap onto my finger and brushed my teeth. It tasted horrible but it was better than night-zombie breath.

"Where are we going?" I asked again when I came out.

"Just in the backyard. You'll be able to hear Tommy if he needs you."

"He'll be fine. He has his inhaler next to him. He used it right before he went to sleep."

I followed him into the yard. We walked across the belly of the skateboard half-pipe. He wore flip-flops. They made funny duck sounds against his heels. When we reached a grove of oak trees, he kicked out of his flip-flops and began climbing up an aluminum ladder propped against a tree. I followed him. When I made it up about ten feet, I saw the platform—about the size of two picnic tabletops bolted together—that had been built between two trees. Little Brew showed me where to put my hands to pull myself up over the edge. He made sure I was settled before he let me go.

"I'm a sky nerd," he said, bending down in the darkness

next to a plastic box. "I'm into the stars. Do you like any of that stuff?"

"I've never really looked at the stars."

"Well," he said, lifting a telescope out of the box and setting it up on a small tripod, "it's a little early in the season for the Perseids, but it's a new moon so we should be able to see some of the Orionids. I just like looking up."

"Awesome. Did you guys build this?"

"When we were smaller. With Dad, actually. We don't really use it anymore. It's just a place to get away from the house. I keep my telescope out here in this box. The platform gives you a little elevation, so you can see out toward the ocean more."

"Do you do this a lot?"

"Often enough. Here," he said, reaching down and handing me a blanket. "If you're cold."

"I'm from New Hampshire," I said. He laughed and took the blanket back and tossed it onto the platform.

"Right," he said, and went back to fiddling with the telescope. He looked through the eyepiece and began adjusting knobs. "I'm a member of an amateur group. I don't know why I like doing it, but I do. A friend of my dad's lives in the Sierra Madres and he has a big telescope. I go up there once or twice a year. He's a star geek, too."

"I think it's great."

"Sky surfing," Little Brew said. "That's what Ty calls it.

I don't sleep all that great so I need something to do at night. Do you want to take a look? I think I've got it now."

My eyes had adjusted, but it was still dark on the platform. Little Brew gave me his hand and I stepped across and bent to the eyepiece. It took me a second to get my vision to work through the telescope. I saw a large white dot with three dashes near the center.

"That's Jupiter," he said, "and some of the moons."

"Amazing."

"It's not much through a small telescope like this. This is just a low-end Meade. The one at my dad's friend's is amazing."

"I'm happy with this," I said, pulling back from the telescope, glancing at him, then looking through the lens again. "Thank you for showing me the stars."

"I'm glad," he said. "I thought you might like this."

"You make me want to look skyward more."

"The Hubble telescope is sending back unbelievable stuff," he said when I straightened. He bent past me to look at Jupiter again. "You can see it online. It's weird, because I don't think most people care. It's like living at a time of exploration and you get to go along with the explorers, and some people can't even be bothered to look."

"Guilty," I said.

"I didn't mean you," he said quickly and looked up. "Honestly, I didn't. I meant all the media and all the stupid reports about movie stars and reality show junk. You have this incredible thing going on and all anyone reads about or watches on television is whether some star is getting a divorce or a belly tuck."

"I see what you mean."

He looked at me and smiled. Then he kissed me. Just like that. It happened so suddenly I didn't quite believe it. I didn't even have time to lift my arms up toward him. Just our lips touched and I felt ready to tip over and fall out of the trees.

"Hope you don't mind," he said, pulling back. "I've wanted to do that since I met you."

"I don't mind," I said.

He kissed me again. Then I kissed him. Jupiter threw whiteness through the eyepiece, like the tiniest light in the world trying to find someplace to rest.

"Your mom keeps calling me," Ty said, pouring me orange juice into a glass. "She kept it up half the night. She's like a stalker woman. The thing kept buzzing on my dresser."

For two guys living together, the kitchen was remarkably clean. Little Brew had gone upstairs and Tommy was still asleep. A few cars started outside and a blue jay screeched at something, probably a cat. Someone drove by with rap music going, the bass pounding.

"Sorry about my mom," I said. "She's just trying to reach Tommy."

"I don't answer but she doesn't stop."

"She's angry and hurt and she's trying to prove she's a concerned mom. It'll stop when we meet up with her. I'll call her after the surfing, anyway."

"That's a relief," Ty said.

We had bagels and butter and strawberry jelly. We also had tea with sugar and plenty of cream. I felt sleep slowly peeling off me, but I wasn't ready to think about Little Brew and our star watching. Not yet. Besides, the sun looked bright and ready. Ty had already made a couple calls to check on conditions. The surf shoot was on. The waves, he said, had been clocked at about thirty feet. The camera crew planned to be there at noon for the best shooting light.

"So what about you, Bee?" Ty asked, sitting across from me. "We haven't really talked about anyone but Tommy. You keep your cards pretty close to your chest."

"I don't mean to," I said. "It's just the way it goes."

"You want to go to college and all that?"

"Dartmouth," I said. "That's my goal. If not Dartmouth, then another Ivy. But Dartmouth is my first choice."

"That means you're a good student," Ty said, biting into his bagel. "Honor roll?"

"Pretty much. I'm a bit obsessive about details. If a teacher assigns something, I get it done. I usually get it finished a few days early. I can't help it."

"And going to Dartmouth will keep you close to Tommy."

"That, too," I said. It was true that I didn't want to be far from my brother. But this trip was making me see that possibilities existed.

"What else do you like to do? For fun, I mean."

"Hang with friends, mostly," I said. "I like movies a lot. Old black-and-white movies from the thirties and forties. Film noir. IMDb is my favorite Web site. I'm always on it. I know, it's odd."

"No it isn't," Ty said. "It's actually pretty cool."

"I like the styles. The women's dresses and things. And the guys all wear suits. It's kind of like a fantasy, only better because it existed. People really did wear those clothes. So that's my dirty little secret."

"How about career stuff?"

"I thought of being a veterinarian for a while. But now I'm thinking of being a doctor. I like the sciences."

"I like the sciences, too," Ty said. "I went to UCLA for marine biology, but then I switched to film. It's a cliché to go to UCLA for film, but that's what I did."

"And this filming today? Is that what you do professionally?"

"Yeah, I have a company called Break Dog," he said,

taking a sip of tea and wiping his mouth. "We make loops of extreme outdoor activities. Boarding, skiing, surfing, motocross, and trick riding. That kind of stuff. We sell subscriptions to places that want a young crowd. They play the loop until it becomes stale or the season changes, then we send them a new one. Eventually I want to do full-length feature films, but this pays the rent right now."

"It's a cool concept."

"Not a real moneymaker, though, but it gives me clips to show people. A way to build the résumé. I like the editing process. Maybe I'll end up being a film editor. Hard to say."

"Things have a way of working out," I said.

He leaned forward a little. And when he spoke, he lowered his voice.

"You think Tommy made you want to be a doctor?" he asked.

"Probably. But maybe I'll change my mind. Do something unexpected."

"You'll be a doctor," Ty said. "Or not. But you'll excel at whatever you choose to do."

I liked Ty, and he was awfully good-looking, but he felt like a big brother. Someone who could mow the grass in front of you without getting into your face. Someone who could also bring over about a thousand good-looking friends. I knew my girlfriends, Jill and Marcie and Maggie, would go nuts over California guys. Cali boys weren't like the ones in New Hampshire. They seemed a lot more relaxed and didn't show off as much. Plus, a lot of them had athletic bodies. I figured it was because they were outside doing things all the time.

"You okay with Tommy going out in the surf today?" Ty asked when he had finished half his bagel. "You don't think it'll be too much, do you?"

"If he goes under, he won't be able to catch his breath."

"I know," Ty said. "We're going to take an easy wave and he's going to ride on my back. We'll have the Jet Ski at the ready to scoop him up."

"It scares me," I said. "I'll be honest. But it's the biggest thing to ever happen to him."

He nodded.

"I'd never deliberately put him at risk," Ty said. "I love that kid."

"I know you do," I said, lowering my voice a little in case Tommy was awake in the next room. "Getting to meet you has meant everything. You don't even know."

"He didn't like that boat trip, did he?" he said, matching the level of my voice. "He didn't say much when I asked him about it, but I could tell. When he e-mailed that his wish was to dive with great whites, I got worried. I figured it would be kind of touristy. Nothing wrong with diving with great whites, but it's not what he's about, exactly. It just didn't seem a match."

"He needed *this*," I said, gesturing around me. "He needed you guys, the way you are. He needed that."

"I like hanging with him. He never complains."

"Never," I confirmed, feeling my throat tighten.

Ty nodded. He finished his bagel before I had finished half of mine. He tidied up and stacked some dishes in the dishwasher. Little Brew came into the kitchen as Ty sat down to sip more tea. Ty glanced at both of us, nodded at something he observed, then lifted his mug. Little Brew passed behind me on the way to the stove, and his hand trailed softly across my shoulders.

After he woke up and had a bagel, Tommy spent an hour with the vest, and this time the guys let him sit quietly. They understood he needed to be in the best shape possible for surfing. Tommy sat and watched television, his arms out, his chest sounding gummy and loose. Ty made last-minute phone calls, lining up elements of the shoot and confirming which friends would be surfing. Little Brew grabbed me and brought me outside to pack the van.

"It was nice last night," he said, lifting a surfboard onto the roof rack. I held the back end while he pushed it forward. "Are you cool with Tommy knowing we like each other?"

"Sure. I think he already knows."

"I like you, Bee. I wish you lived closer."

"So do I."

He climbed up on the bumper and used ratchet straps to tie down the board. Then we grabbed another board and carried it over to the back of the van. This one felt heavier and denser.

"Lots of girls around here are into the malls and all that ridiculous stuff," he said. "You're not like that."

"Well, to be fair, we don't even have a mall in my part of New Hampshire."

"That's what I mean," he said. "I've never met an Eastern girl before."

Then he asked me to push the back of the surfboard harder while he guided it into place. He climbed onto the bumper and used a second ratchet strap to tie it down. We had four boards piled on top and a bunch of gear—wet suits, cameras, life jackets, and so on—jumbled in the back of the van. He had to wrestle the last board into place twice before he was finally satisfied with it. By the time he jumped down, Ty came out and joined us.

"We've got it set," Ty said. "We have to get moving, though. Tommy says he's done."

"He's good to go, then," I said.

"You should bring your things, so that I can run you up to San Francisco after. Either the hotel or the airport."

"How long does the shoot take?"

"A couple hours, maybe. It depends on the light and what the waves are doing. We do mostly handheld shots, so we can film in all conditions. We'll see."

"I'll get Tommy," I said.

Ty and Little Brew did one last check of the gear while I rounded up Tommy. His color looked bad. Part of it might have been the television light, but he looked jaundiced and thin and it took him a second to find his voice after I unstrapped the vest. I pushed back his hair and looked at his eyes. He felt warm. He jerked his head to one side to get my hand off. He tried to get up, but the couch cushions were too deep.

"Are you feeling okay?" I asked Tommy. "You feel warm."

"Yes, Bee's Knees," he said. "I'm fine."

I got him onto his feet. He clicked the remote at the television. He had to click a couple times before it finally hissed closed. He tossed the remote onto the couch.

"I'm doing this," he said. "Nothing's stopping me."

"No one is saying you can't. We just have to be smart."

He shrugged. And because he's Tommy, he slowly nodded.

"Okay," he said. "I know you're a little worried."

"You have to promise you'll be honest and tell me if it feels like too much, okay? No one's going to judge you. These guys like you just the way you are."

He nodded again. I told him Ty had promised to drive us back to San Francisco later. Then he helped me collect our things. We didn't have much. By the time we had shoved everything into our backpacks, Little Brew and Ty had finished with the equipment check. The sun threw hard shadows straight down at us.

"Thirty-footers!" Little Brew said when he saw Tommy. "The surfing Snow Pony."

Tommy struck a pose as if he were surfing. It looked ridiculous.

"We're ready," Ty said, closing the rear doors to the van. "You guys all set?"

"We're set," I said.

I helped Tommy inside. Watching him climb into the shotgun spot—lift the leg, organize his weight, rock forward, miss, rock forward again, then semicollapse inside—I had a moment of doubt. The whole idea seemed crazy. I pictured him out in the waves, or worse, below, down in the swirl of water and sand, his frail body beaten and turned every which way. I wondered if I wasn't being irresponsible. *Of course* Tommy wanted to surf. *Of course* he thought it would be cool and fun and only a little dangerous. But I was supposed to keep an eye on him.

"Let's roll," Ty yelled.

Little Brew hopped in, his skin already coated with

sunblock. He reached forward and tapped Tommy's head. Tommy turned and tried to fight back, but his movement was impossibly slow, a frog tongue after an insect that had already darted off.

"Perfect day," Ty said, pulling things out of the back as I helped Tommy down from the shotgun seat. Ty used a small plastic wagon to carry stuff. He filled it quickly.

Water sparkled blue and sharp everywhere to our west. The sand on Half Moon Bay State Beach looked dry and crisp. A clutter of people had erected their umbrellas a little farther down the beach. Now and then, depending on the wind, we heard them yell and scream. Someone hit a baseball with an aluminum bat and the odd *plink* carried better than anything else. The sea and waves rolled in, rinsing back through the sand.

A sign next to the parking lot warned surfers.

ATTENTION
Mavericks Break requires advanced
water skills. DO NOT attempt to
surf or Jet Ski these waves unless
you are experienced. Possibility of
drowning is real and present. In case
of emergency, call 911.

"Mark Foo drowned here," Tommy said, spotting the sign and walking over to inspect it. "He was a world-class big-wave rider from Hawaii. He got trapped underneath, they think, but no one really knows. He might have been knocked unconscious by his board."

"Don't be putting any mumbo jumbo on us," Little Brew said, loud enough for Tommy to hear. "Get over here and give us a hand. You two need to put on some wet suits."

"Where are the Jet Skis?" I asked, putting my hand up to shade my eyes.

"They'll be here," Ty said, still off-loading equipment. "They launch a little ways north and ride in. We have two of them. You and Little Brew can go on one."

"And the cameras?" I asked.

"Some are with the Jet Skis."

Unloading took a while. Ty made Little Brew ferry the equipment in the wagon to the edge of the water. Meanwhile, he scrambled up onto the van roof and unhitched the surfboards. After we squeezed into wet suits, Tommy and I helped him place the boards on the beach. Dunes and headlands rose to the north. By the time Little Brew arrived back at the van, Ty had everything ready. I smeared sunblock on Tommy's face. He hated me for it.

"Stoked?" Ty asked Tommy. "You ready to ride some mad barrels?"

"I'm stoked," Tommy said. "Definitely."

"I saw Ollie and Honey," Little Brew said. "They're already out on the Jet Skis."

"What about Florence?"

"She's not coming," Little Brew said. "Honey said she sprained her ankle." He looked at me. "Florence is an awesome surfer," he explained. "Ty has a crush on her."

Then a strange moment arrived. Everyone turned to Tommy. It seemed to occur to all of us that he could easily be in over his head. It was one thing to consider putting him in the water when we had proposed it on land, but now with the water a hundred yards off, the sound of the surf chucking against the beach, it was difficult to believe this made any sense at all. I glanced at Ty. Little Brew stood with a funny grin on his face. Tommy didn't notice. He began marching toward the waterline, his gait clumsy and slow, his small back fragile and no wider than a baseball glove.

TOMMY SHARK FACT #8: In the spring of 1961, three surfers, Alex Matienzo, Jim Thompson, and Dick Knottmeyer, decided to try the distant waves off Pillar Point on the Northern California Coast. A white-haired German shepherd swam out with them, but the conditions were too rough for the dog. The dog, who belonged to Matienzo, was named Maverick, and the surfers eventually brought him back in and tied him to the bumper of their car. The dog gave his name to the huge waves that broke over a reef nearly two miles out to sea. No one else surfed "Mavericks" until Jeff Clark came along. He was a local kid who surfed alone on Mavericks for fifteen years. He didn't purposely keep the waves a secret, but few people imagined that waves of such power existed off Pillar Point.

A fisherman once pulled out three great whites off Pillar Point in a single day. An article written by Ben Marcus in *Surfer* described Mavericks as "gloomy, isolated, inherently evil. The reef is surrounded by deep water, and lies naked to every nasty thing above and below the Pacific: Aleutian swells, northwest winds, southeast storms, frigid currents, aggro elephant seals and wilder things that snack on aggro elephant seals. . . . Mavericks radiates danger."

● ● ●

I had a weird moment as we carried stuff to the beach. I felt light-headed and slightly out of my body. I could see myself performing the task of lifting a bag and setting down my end of the surfboard, but I couldn't sense myself experiencing it. It's hard to describe. Mixed in with it was a feeling of déjà vu. Somehow it felt as if I had done this exact thing before, that I had been to Mavericks, that I had sat on the high headland to the north and watched the waves break and shatter on their run in from Alaska. Even the squawk of the gulls, just for an instant, became garbled and melancholy, like someone talking through a curtain at me. I could nearly make out what they were saying, but the words scrambled away just on the verge of my understanding. The sun beat down and the sand felt warm under my feet, which only made things more confusing. I should have been happy to be in the sunshine, but instead I felt as though a phone was ringing somewhere, an important call coming in, and I couldn't get to it. Things moved too slowly, or appeared magically, and I wondered if I had eaten enough, if my blood sugar had dropped somehow. And then for a second, I experienced clarity.

My mom had once made a kaleidoscope out of quartz and glass, and I used to like looking through it before Tommy broke it by accident. Anyway, there was something sliced and jagged about the way the world appeared. Tommy noticed my glazed look and asked me twice if I was okay, and I said yes, but I didn't feel that way. Then I put my hand on Little Brew's shoulder, and his skin felt so warm and smooth. As he turned to me and smiled, the world came back into focus and the sun became merely the sun again, and the ocean began making sound again. I was on a beach in California, and I was hot and probably thirsty, and the day felt peaceful.

Little Brew pulled my hand around until he had me directly in front of him. And he kissed me.

Water. Mounds and mountains of water. I sat on the Jet Ski behind Little Brew and watched the swells roll slowly toward the Maverick break. I had never seen anything like it. I had never felt anything like it. On a boat the sea is another road, a path, a surface. But when I was sitting behind Little Brew, the Jet Ski bubbling and impatient to get going, the ocean was no longer abstract. It was undeniably *here*, all around, above and below, melted to the sky and angry at the land. The sun reflected light everywhere, scalding and bright, and far away, back near land, the scent of trees and dirt and rocks came to us every now and then. The five surfers — Ty in the middle — sat on their surfboards, their bodies half turned, their faces expectant and nervous and intently fixed on the advancing water.

When all was said and done, the waves did not approach thirty feet. They might have been ten feet, maybe less, but they still rolled toward us with an urgency and power that made me feel small and insignificant. Ollie — a guy about Ty's age, but shorter and stockier with black hair that curled and fell every which way — rode on a second Jet Ski. Tommy rode behind him. Ollie held a camera and acted more or less as a director. He and Ty had already discussed the shoot and knew what they wanted. I wondered, though, how anyone could believe in a plan in the face of so much water.

"We ready?" Ty yelled to Ollie.

Ollie nodded and held his thumb up. It was one o'clock, maybe one-thirty. I looked around Little Brew to spot Tommy. Tommy wore a bright orange life jacket over his wet suit. The jacket looked too big for him. He appeared even smaller than usual in the swell of the ocean. His expression hadn't changed since we left the shoreline. He smiled at everything. I had never seen him smile so much.

I caught his eye and raised my eyebrow to ask if he was okay. He looked away without responding.

Then, suddenly, Little Brew gave the Jet Ski gas, and we darted fifty feet in toward shore, parallel to the waves but removed from their force. I kept my arms tight around his waist. One of the surfers, a teenager named Willy, had paddled to the ledge. He was in position to catch a wave. The other guys watched.

It was beautiful.

For a minute or two, Willy sat on his board studying the waves. Then, at a point that made sense to him, he lay out on his board and began paddling hard. I saw his target wave. It had arrived from Alaska, a trillion molecules colliding and shivering with energy, the form determined by forces nearly unimaginable. The bottom of the ocean caused the wave to bulge. That was something I had never understood before, not as I understood it now, because I watched it push up as surely as a balloon expanding and lifting, pressure from the bottom exerting force, cutting the lower sections of the waves away so that the top became heavier and heavier. A single thread of water, frayed and delicate, flickered at the top. The gut of the wave, though, pushed its belly forward and for a second it didn't seem as though it would break. But it had to break, and Willy, sensing the speed, feeling his board lift, paddled harder, kicking, too, until he achieved a moment's balance where the wave, more than he, had to decide whether to carry him forward or release him. Watching him, I wondered what was going through his head. What did he think—or did he think at all?—as the water lifted him, sped him forward, his board becoming a torpedo, his hands moving to the gunwales and gripping. I heard the wave begin to hiss and moan, and then whatever was about to happen had to happen. Nothing could prevent it, because the wave had pushed up at the sky, glinting and formidable, the taste of open ocean suddenly in the air, oxygen everywhere, and then Willy popped.

He popped.

With one motion, his arms and legs two halves of a pair of tongs snapping shut, his waist the anchoring point, he shot up onto his feet. Quick. Smooth. He teetered for a second and nearly went over, but then he aimed the board down, down, and I realized that the wave had grown without my seeing it. It had built to ten feet, the size and width of a tree falling, and suddenly, in a sort of New Hampshire way, I comprehended that the energy of a wave was similar to the energy of a tree falling through space, the bottom pinned, the top branches building in speed as it approached the earth. The water had tripped on a stone beneath it and was falling recklessly forward.

Little Brew made a whooping sound as Willy shot down the wave and cut right.

He came toward us. For an instant we saw him inside the wave. His knees flexed, his hands out for balance, he rode in the barrel, sun turning the water above him tea-colored, the white rip of the wave sending damp sparks into the air. Joy. I saw joy pass over his face; he had nailed the wave, caught it, and the board cut across the slope of the water, faster and faster, the wave no longer angry or intent, but simply following physics. Joy and grace. Then, in a quick shove, he stuck his feet down, rocked backward, and the board cut up the front of the wave and shot him off its back. Willy flew into the air, peeling back over the wave, and the board and his body exploded into space. He went seven feet, ten feet into the air, drifting like a cartoon character, and before he landed we were buzzing forward to his landing spot, shooting in to pluck him out before the next wave could begin to stumble.

"You're next!" Little Brew yelled.

It took me a three-count to realize he meant me.

"I don't think so," I said, but Little Brew didn't listen.

Willy had been fine. He had paddled off by himself, skirting around the center of the waves when another surfer, Honey, came gliding down the face of a ten-footer. Honey didn't have it, though. I knew it as soon as I saw it. He leaned a little forward once he gained his feet, and the nose of the board traveled too fast. It traveled and bucked and pretty soon he dove off the front, dangerously, and the board flipped and followed him. Then the wave caught him, crushing and rinsing, and we lost sight of him altogether. The wave continued to grind and Little Brew expertly navigated the white wash, swooping in to check on Honey. He had to be mindful of coming in too fast, of barging over a surfer in the water, but he had a good eye and by the time Honey rose to the surface, his wet suit glinting, his face turned in a frown momentarily, we idled fifteen feet from him.

"Okay?" Little Brew yelled.

Honey nodded and hoisted himself back onto the board. Another wave began pouring down on us, its gallop of white and foam pushing forward and already rebuilding into a wave that would eventually break on the shore.

Under all this, sharks. Under us, the great white swimming and eyeing the seal-shaped boards.

TOMMY SHARK FACT #9: No one knows how long a great white shark lives. Some biologists think thirty years. Others—on the margin among researchers—say a great white can live as long as seventy years. Besides questions about their longevity, biologists also know little about the great whites' sex life. When sharks return to the Farallon Islands, for example, the females often have bite marks near their heads. Whether that's part of the mating ritual, no one can say for sure. No one has seen a great white mate. Tagging records suggest that the Farallon sharks spend the winter off Mexico in one of the deepest parts of the Pacific, and it's possible that the mating takes place in the deep blue waters of the tropics. The round trip from the Farallones to the deep Mexican waters is approximately two thousand miles. Several things about this behavior astonish scientists. First, the pure distance involved is impressive, especially because it appears the fuel needed for such a journey is captured in a small window of time very close to shore during the late-autumn seal run. The energy efficiency of the sharks' swimming and navigation must be extraordinary in order to carry off such a trip.

Further, it's peculiar that a creature that feeds so close to shore disappears into the deep and does not seem to feed in a sustainable way until it returns to the Farallones. The sharks appear thin and hungry when they make it back, and the seals suffer decapitation and constant attack until the sharks fill their stomachs once more. *Rapacious*, Tommy has said, liking the big word. *Rapacious*.

●　●　●

"You're up," Little Brew yelled. "Hop in and swim over."

"I'm not feeling it," I said. "It wasn't part of the plan. I don't think I can do it."

"Sure you can. Just go with the flow. We have you."

It seemed like a crazy idea. It seemed like the worst idea in the world to jump into the water in the middle of the ocean.

"Bee," Tommy shouted, his voice hardly loud enough to carry over the sound of the waves. "You're holding things up. We're on a schedule."

So I jumped. Clumsily, but I did it. Beneath me, a thousand feet, a million feet of water stretched and ripped and pulled. Besides the fact that it was embarrassing to have to climb onto a guy, it also meant that for a moment I became a seal. All the abstract shark information Tommy had fed me over the years suddenly felt concrete. A shark could be underneath us, at least theoretically. We resembled a pod of seals sitting out beyond the breakers, and I could imagine the shark swimming below, its body twisting just a shade to let its black eye peer up at us through the shimmering waves. Food or not food? Correct shape or incorrect shape? A mammal in a slick black wet suit or a piece of marine junk?

I reached Ty's board in two strokes.

"Okay," Ty said, "just kind of slither up on top of me."

"I'll knock you over," I said.

"The board's stable," Ty said calmly. "Just give it a try."

I nodded, not wanting my legs dangling in shark water longer than they had to. Quickly, I went perpendicular to Ty and he reached down and helped me. I hoisted myself up, rising just a little, and then Little Brew boosted me from the Jet Ski. I turned myself lengthwise on the board, fitting myself to Ty's body.

He started to paddle. Little Brew bubbled off on the Jet Ski.

"I can't believe I'm doing this," I said.

"You'll be fine" Ty said.

I wasn't so sure.

Then something clicked. I turned and saw Tommy on the back of Ollie's Jet Ski and he nodded at me. For once he was taking care of me, and all my fear and nervousness drained away. I kept my eyes on Tommy. He continued nodding, encouraging me, and for an instant, I felt that his illness had carved me somehow, had shaped me a little off and made me frightened. It was time to start living, time to look ahead and risk a little. I looked at Tommy one last time—my brother who had gum in his lungs and frail, weak bones, but who had a spirit to bring him across the country and onto the largest surf in California. My mother was right, after all: he studied sharks because he had never been able to swim without wondering what was beneath him, without wondering when the CF would deliver its final blow, and I could not conceive of his courage, his gentle spirit living day after day fighting for breath. I told Ty I was ready and I felt my body grow stronger and then the water lifted. It pushed us up in space, raised us toward the sun as if showing what it could do, what it intended, like a tennis player showing a ball before he served it, and then I felt Ty's body go stiff and hard and he began to paddle. Ty Barry, the guy who had survived a shark attack, who had been bumped five feet into the air, who had watched the gray-white of the seventeen-foot shark swirl beneath him, letting him go, giving him life. I knew I could be with no one safer. He could not be twice jinxed.

"We got it, we got it, we got it!" he yelled.

I heard my own voice go crazy in a scream of delight, and then the wave began to build and build and build. Each end of the wave tightened, and up we went, up, more, until Ty nodded, and I hugged closer to him and felt the world start to tilt.

"Here we go!" Ty shouted.

And we did.

We caught the edge of the wave, tipped forward, and then shot down the face, angling a little right, the wave driving us. The wave no longer cared about us, I realized. It was now just physics, just the end of one rhythm and one motion unleashed thousands of miles north of where we lay on a bright red board and arced down and down and down. For a second the wave collapsed on us and I thought it was over, we were crushed, but then we shot forward again, took the wave's energy and rode it away from itself, and we felt like a tongue, like a bright poke of joy, and the wave had to hurry to reach us. But it did. It crashed over my legs, which was all right because the buoyancy of the board made us go faster, and then Ty began pulling out. I'm not sure how I knew that but I did, and he torqued his shoulder into the wave and we began to climb up. For an instant I saw blue sky, great white clouds, and then the wave finally rolled us. It slammed us down, and then Ty was gone, and the board knocked my shin and disappeared, and I was under, under, under. I waited and performed a slow somersault, and then the wave, the violence that was once a wave, passed. It let me go without a struggle and I swam up, up, up and crashed through the surface of the water. I raised my fist and I pumped it and I shouted and Little Brew swung by and yanked me onto the back of the Jet Ski. He grabbed me and kissed him and I kissed him, couldn't stop kissing him, and Tommy yelled, "Wooooo-hoooo!" When I looked behind us, Ty was already back on the board paddling after us, and the waves kept throwing themselves at the sky, and failing, and trying again.

Tommy stepped off the back of Ollie's Jet Ski and fell straight down into the water, his life jacket making him bob vertically in the rolling swells. The water was too big. It was too big for such a small boy and we all sensed it, I did, anyway, and I watched with my heart stopping to see him struggle the few feet to Ty's board.

"Snow Pony!" Little Brew yelled, trying to buck Tommy up. He brought our Jet Ski close to Ty's board. Ollie filmed. I held Little Brew with all my might.

The other guys—Willy and Honey and two more boys whose names I didn't quite catch—circled Ty's board. It was obvious they had all talked about Tommy's condition and they all tried to help. Tommy ignored them. I saw his jaw set as he tried to climb up onto Ty's board as I had done, but his arms were too weak and his life jacket blocked him with its bulk. Little Brew bent down off our Jet Ski and helped Tommy get a lift; then Honey came over and let Tommy use his board as a second point of balance, and with everyone helping, Tommy finally clambered onto Ty's back. Little Brew gave out a whoop, but you could tell it was forced.

I wanted to stop Tommy. It wasn't a good idea to let him run the waves. I knew it. Everyone there suddenly knew it, but we couldn't stop the momentum. The sun still shone and the water glinted. The waves still built and broke, built and broke, but we were farther out to sea and the breakers held no threat for us.

Then Tommy surprised us all.

With extraordinary effort, he pushed himself onto his knees. Then, inch by inch, he lifted the top half of his body so that he knelt on Ty's back, his hands slowly leaving the safety of the board, his tiny, stunted body trembling with the effort. He raised himself, only for second, but for that second he surfed as others surfed. He stood, as much as he could, proving something to himself. I felt everyone grow still, and my eyes began to tear, and Tommy lifted himself again, lamely, twice raising his body to prove he could surf, and he didn't do it for show, but to have one instant of confirmation. He was a boy and he was on a surfboard and he did not want to be the sickly kid. But he was, of course, and that was in his movement, too, and Little Brew shouted again, this time for real, and the other guys joined in and revved him up, shouting about *the Snow Pony, the Tommymeister, the Surf-dude.* I yelled, too, yelled until my throat hurt, because Tommy was a surfer, his heart knew it even if his body didn't, and when he spread back out against Ty, he nodded and said he was ready to go.

Little Brew brought us around to a vantage point where we could watch. Ollie came to rest beside us and got the camera ready. Minutes later we saw Ty paddle for a wave and he and Tommy caught it easily. It was not an enormous wave. They rose above us, the wave teetering, and I saw Tommy's small arms paddling, too, helping Ty even though the help was not needed or effective. Then Ty stopped and the board sloped down and to the right, and the wave began to curl on top of them. I saw Tommy's face then. His face locked in joy and triumph, and it did not change even when I saw the board dip and begin to turn. The wave crashed down on them and for a second they outran it, but then the board got too far down and gave the wave a chance to swipe them with the flat of its broad body. Down they went. The board submerged and I saw Ty slide off, then Tommy; it reminded me of kids falling off a toboggan, except the water closed over them and the wave broke and a gull squawked loudly just off to the seaward side.

Little Brew shot us forward. He topped the last rise of Tommy's wave and gunned us down into the valley between the dying wave and the mounting one. I held my breath. An instant later I saw Ty pop onto his board, his hand up to say he was fine, and I heard Little Brew rev down the engine because he wasn't sure where to go.

I didn't see Tommy.

No one saw Tommy.

"Oh, no, no, no, no, no," I whispered, my eyes running up and down over the surf, in the waves, everywhere. "Oh, no."

Then Ollie yelled and Little Brew turned around to see where Ollie was pointing, and I followed the line of Ollie's arm, too. Tommy rode in the wash of the wave, his arm up, the orange jacket keeping him buoyant. The wave had carried him closer to shore than we anticipated, and Little Brew flashed us forward, gunning it wildly, and I saw that he put us at risk because the building wave chased us. But if Little Brew didn't catch him, then Tommy would have to endure a second wave crashing on top of him. Even as Little Brew surged us forward, I saw Tommy begin to be sucked into the draw of the approaching wave. The collision became inevitable. Little Brew could not reach him in time, so he gunned us out of the waves and shot southward, positioning himself to be ready for the next wash. And we watched as Tommy got sucked into the curl of the new wave, his head a brown dot in an absurdly large swell of water. The wave snapped down, smacking against the water below it. I covered my eyes as Tommy disappeared again.

The wave seemed to flutter forever. It frothed and blew spray into the air and in all the whiteness we saw nothing of Tommy. I screamed—later they told me I screamed—but I wasn't conscious of it. I willed the wave to stop, but that was foolish, and only when the force of the wave had extinguished itself on the slack water below it did I see Tommy's head bobbing in the froth of water racing toward the beach.

"There!" I yelled.

Everyone yelled.

Little Brew was on it. He gunned the Jet Ski until it made a high, whining-mosquito sound. I held on to him, my nails digging into his belly. He reached Tommy in a flash, and, with relief, I saw Tommy's hand come up. But it wasn't as easy as that. Little Brew had to lean way off the Jet Ski to help Tommy aboard, and before he could get him up a new wave began to collapse toward us. I could tell that Tommy was spent. In contrast, Little Brew's movements grew desperate. He yanked and pulled, and I clawed at Tommy to get him on the seat between us while the wave to seaward began to draw us toward it. Then Tommy succeeded in flopping across the seat in front of Little Brew—I wasn't sure how—and Little Brew jerked the Jet Ski into a full run. Tommy's legs skimmed the surface and he slid partially off, but Little Brew held on to him. I held on to Little Brew. The wave behind began to sprint at us, spilling and gleaming like a murderous teardrop, and for a second it became a race again. Tommy slid farther off the Jet Ski until half his body dragged in the foamy water, and Little Brew throttled down to keep him connected. I reached out and grabbed Tommy's jacket, then the wave broke and we disappeared in the wash of spray and turbulence. My hand lost its grip on Tommy. I said *no, no, no* again under my breath and closed my eyes. I couldn't watch if it meant watching us lose Tommy a second time. I couldn't stand to see it. But then the throb of the Jet Ski caught my ears and I opened my eyes and saw Little Brew steering with his right hand, his left locked onto Tommy's life jacket.

"Hold on," Little Brew yelled to me, to Tommy, to anyone who could hear him.

He shot us forward, buzzing through the wash, the water shooting out the back like a rooster tail. I looked around Little Brew and saw immediately that Tommy's color was horrible. When he saw me, his eyes half closed, Tommy made the choke motion.

"He can't breathe! He can't breathe!" I shouted. "Get him to shore!"

Little Brew glanced back at me, not quite understanding.

"Now, now, he can't breathe!" I screamed. "He needs medicine."

Little Brew nodded. He grabbed Tommy tighter and shot forward, running the waves and the wash expertly while Ollie followed behind us, the waves trying to rock us back off shore.

I saw a shark as we brought Tommy in.

I saw it five feet underwater, maybe more. It passed like a blue-black piece of sealskin, its dorsal fin grazing the surface. Ollie didn't see it. Neither did Little Brew nor Tommy. But I did. Somehow it felt as though I had been waiting to see it my entire life.

It cruised near the surface, its body longer than the Jet Ski, three times as long, and it passed in a hurried way. The shark was going somewhere. It rolled slightly on its starboard side, its eye lifting to meet mine. I was not food at that moment. I witnessed the shark's panic, its fright at something—maybe the Jet Ski—and saw it pass quickly into the deeper elements. It glided down, all efficiency, and the thresher cut of its tail flicked twice and sent it straight under the waves. Except for the buggy hum of the Jet Skis, the sea had gone quiet—the gulls and the wind. The shark seemed to carry all sound with it.

Little Brew ran his Jet Ski as close to the shore as possible, but he couldn't jam it up onto the beach because Tommy's legs still trailed in the water. He stopped ten feet out and Ollie jumped off right behind him and together they hoisted Tommy onto the sand. I ran past them, heading for my backpack, and I dug around until I found the inhaler. I ran back and squeezed between them and slipped my hand under Tommy's head. His eyes didn't open; his chest didn't move. I pried the mouthpiece between his lips and depressed the plunger.

"Call nine-one-one," I said, my voice surprisingly calm. "Do it now."

"I don't have a phone," Little Brew said.

"Run up the beach. Find someone. Call nine-one-one."

Little Brew ran off. I turned to Ollie.

"I saw a shark on the way in," I said. "Go tell those guys."

He looked at me, confused.

"A shark," I said. "A great white."

"Okay," he said.

"Go tell them. Get them in."

I bent down and whispered into Tommy's ear.

"I saw a shark," I said.

He didn't breathe. I put my ear to his lips. No air passed in or out of his lungs. I listened to Ollie start his Jet Ski. I heard it whine out into the surf. After a short while, its whine gave way to the wail of approaching sirens. I pressed Tommy's chest lightly and pushed down, thinking I could get his lungs working. His left eyelid flickered, but that was all. A reef of sand ringed his chin and I saw where the life jacket had abraded his neck and jawline, rubbing itself in a shrug while it carried him through the surf.

"They're on the way," Little Brew said, falling to the sand beside us. "A lady had already called when she saw us."

I nodded. I turned Tommy's head. A drizzle of water spilled out of his mouth. It came slowly, almost reluctantly, like a bottle leaking. I brought his face back up and bent down and put my mouth over Tommy's and breathed. I wasn't sure how to do it. "Tilt his chin back," Little Brew said. I did.

I blew hard into Tommy's lungs, my mouth sealed around his, and I counted and did it over and over. The count changed each time. Sometimes I could do it with a proper cadence, and sometimes I breathed too quickly. Little Brew carefully straightened Tommy's legs. It made no difference, but he did it anyway.

Then, suddenly, black trousers appeared—I did not look up, I kept my eyes on Tommy—and a pair of hands moved me away. I told them the details: *cystic fibrosis, surfing, no Pulmozyme, no air, Tommy, his name is Tommy, my brother, I'm responsible, Tommy, New Hampshire, yes, I don't know, eleven years old, not this bad, not before, yes, probably, his mother is in San Francisco, our mother, I saw a shark, yes, just beyond the surf line, Tommy, my name is Bee.*

The paramedics took him, a breathing nipple already inserted in Tommy's lips, the squawk and static of radio communications building and sizzling, feverish. I stayed beside the stretcher until they climbed up the sandy hill and put him into the back of the ambulance. Tommy looked like a small newborn on the big white cot. His face looked calm and flat and tired. I tried to climb in beside him, but I wasn't allowed. Someone kicked the siren into high and it whooped. A paramedic with white rubber gloves handed me a card and said to follow.

Ty appeared at my shoulder.

"I'll take you, Bee. Come on."

Ollie had my backpack. He handed it to me. Little Brew and Ty ran on either side of me. The van had turned into a furnace sitting in the sun. It felt strange to get into such heat after the cold water. When Little Brew began to roll down the windows, I asked him to keep them up. Even in the wet suit I was shivering. The heat helped against the shivering.

Ty broke down.

He broke down at the first light we hit and he began to sob. He bent his head over the steering wheel and covered his face with his hands. I wanted to say something comforting, but I couldn't speak. I reached a hand over and put it on his shoulder. He didn't acknowledge it. When the light changed, Little Brew tapped him on the other shoulder and said to get going. Ty shook himself and drove. The traffic didn't move very well. The afternoon had slipped toward evening and people were headed home, running errands or fooling around on a day off. The quiet from the middle of the day was over.

"I saw a shark," I said at the next light.

Ty nodded. Little Brew let air out of his lungs in a long sigh.

"It was big and dark," I said. "And it was running from something. Or it was swimming fast. It was a white."

No one said anything. Then the light changed and Ty started driving again. We drove and let the heat cook us until finally we opened the windows and let the day inside. A pair of flies buzzed at the top of the van, swimming in heat, their bodies like sparks clicking against the roof.

"There's been an accident," I whispered into the phone.

"Where are you, Bee?" my mother asked.

"Tommy . . . ," I said.

"Where are you? Tell me immediately."

"Sequoia Hospital in Redwood City."

"And Half Moon is south of here?"

"Yes," I said.

"And what's happened?"

"Tommy went under the water," I said. "He couldn't get out of the waves."

"Bee," she said, her voice going tight and hard, "what are you telling me?"

"We're at the hospital."

"But he'll be okay," she said.

"I don't know."

"Bee?"

"Hurry," I said.

"You have so much to answer for," she said, but I heard her pulling things together into a bag. "I've been beside myself."

"He's hurt, Mom."

"Is there a doctor there? I need to speak to whoever is in charge."

"We're in the waiting room. No one's here right now. No one to talk to, I mean."

"I will be there as fast as humanly possible. Can I reach you at this number?"

"Yes," I said.

"You answer the darn phone if I call, do you hear me?"

"Yes," I said.

"Bee, didn't I tell you he isn't strong enough for this kind of thing?"

"You don't even know what kind of thing it was," I said. "Mom, just get here."

She didn't say anything. I heard her doing something that made her bracelets clink. Her breathing went away from the speaker, then returned a second later.

"I'm packed. I'm checking out and coming down there. Do not move. Stay right where you are."

"We will," I said.

"Tell him I love him."

"I haven't seen him yet."

"Are you saying he's dead, Bee?"

Her voice went up and teetered somewhere.

"I don't know. He wasn't breathing."

"Oh, Lord. Not Tommy," she said.

"Hurry."

"You call me instantly if you hear anything," she said.

"I will."

I heard a door close. Then she started walking. I heard her heels.

"This is really irresponsible behavior on your part. Inexcusable."

"I agree," I said. "I hate myself right now."

"You should not encourage him."

"I'm sorry, Mom."

"He looks up to you."

"Hurry."

"Okay, I'll be there as soon as I can. Just hold on."

She didn't hang up, though. She didn't talk, either. I listened to her go to the front desk, throw her key card into someone's hand, explain in a single statement she was checking out, then continue on, her heels like hammer blows across the tile floor. I heard the bag on wheels she pulled behind her, then heard it change pitch as she made it onto the cement walkway outside. Maybe then the phone did something to draw her attention, because she clicked off.

"Did you really see a shark?" Little Brew whispered to me.

We were sitting in the waiting room. I wore a towel around my waist and a T-shirt on top, and Little Brew wore his baggy shorts and nothing else. None of us had changed because we expected to hear something about Tommy any second. The air-conditioning felt cold. Ty had gone out to park the van in a different place. He thought he would get a ticket if he left it where he had first parked it. A coffee machine sat on top of a small refrigerator, which hummed and bumped now and then. It felt as though the day had gone to stay somewhere else and we were left to wait for it.

I nodded about the shark.

"What a freaky day," Little Brew said, shaking his head. "A crazy day."

"It was dark, not white. People say they're white sharks, but they aren't. They're dark on top. Tommy said they suntan."

"I never knew that," Little Brew said.

"Tommy knows everything about sharks," I said.

Little Brew nodded. Something inside told me I should keep talking about sharks. If I did, somehow their power would pass along to Tommy.

Ty came back a few minutes later. He had moved the van, which he told us about in more detail than we needed, simply to keep the silence from closing in on us. Little Brew said I was serious about seeing a shark, and Ty nodded. He sat down and tapped his feet a little. A line of sand had collected in the hairs along his calves. More crystals of sand or salt ran under his right eye.

"Ollie reported your sighting," Little Brew said, his skin raised in gooseflesh. "Some of the other guys ignored the warning, but that was just a macho thing. Ollie told people on the beach, too."

"Good," I said.

"They'll probably clear people out and send a chopper over," Little Brew went on. "Some folks on the beach thought the whole thing with Tommy was a shark attack. They got it mixed up."

"Okay," Ty said, which was his way of telling Little Brew to be quiet.

We sat for a while. No one spoke. A boy with a round belly and a cast on his leg limped past and pushed through a double door. A nurse came by carrying a tray with a handkerchief over it. No one was supposed to see what was under the handkerchief. Somewhere deeper in the building a drill ran for a minute or so, the sound going high like a dentist finding a cavity. When the sound cut off, a dog began barking out in the parking lot. The drill sound kept jumping around and ricocheting in my skull even after it had shut off.

I stood. I walked to the double doors. It had been too long. I pushed through the doors and walked straight ahead. I wasn't sure where to go. I passed a nurses' station and kept going. Someone moaned in one of the rooms. A spine of fluorescent lights hung overhead.

"Miss?" a female voice said, but I kept going.

I had to keep walking. If I didn't keep walking I would crumple. Tommy was somewhere in the hospital wing and I had to find him. An orderly pushing a large machine came at me from the other direction. We nodded at each other. And the woman who had called *Miss* called it again. This time I heard quick footsteps follow the word. But I had found Tommy's room. I knew Tommy was inside be-cause the orange life jacket lay on a wheeled tray outside the door. The straps had been cut. The jacket was opened like a trout filleted and spread on an iron skillet.

The sight of the life vest stopped me. I didn't dare move forward or look away. Suddenly the woman who had said *Miss* grabbed my elbow. When I turned, I saw a large woman with too much makeup and hair the color of rusted oil barrels.

"You can't be in this area, sweetie," she said.

"My brother's in there," I said. "In that room."

"We're doing everything we can," she said, squeezing my elbow a little to get me going.

But I snapped away and took the few steps I needed to look into Tommy's room. I spotted him almost at once, his face framed by the shoulders of three or four doctors squaring around the bed. They had strapped something into his mouth and the sheets had been pulled up to his chin. Before I could do anything, I heard my mother call to me.

"Bee?" she said.

She came down the hall quickly, her heels whacking the tile. I turned and fell into her, sobs coming from deeper than anyplace I knew about. She put her arms around me and held me. The boy with the cast limped by but didn't look. He kept his eyes forward and concentrated on walking.

The changing light in the waiting room, shadows tracking the hours across the floor. Venetian blinds, dusty gray-green, moving slightly in the breeze from the air conditioner. Two slats crooked. The television off and silent. Mom and the boys, her annoyance palpable. Her greeting and awareness of them short and curt, her deep, final sigh, whispering *What were you all thinking?* Time passing. The swinging doors popping open, drawing our looks, then swinging closed with someone new on the other side. A nurse, a patient, not Tommy. A buzz from a fluorescent lamp. The scent of coffee and sugar. The short, tight click of an electric clock against the wall and a fly, leisurely ticking along the windowpane.

Finally, a voice confirming our name, asking my mom and me to follow. Ty onto his feet. Little Brew squeezing my hand and nodding encouragement as I left him. A nurse walking on white shoes, a colorful smock, a blood-pressure gauge tucked in her hip pocket. The squeak of her sneaker tread when she rounds the corner almost athletic, almost winter nights in a gym with snow falling outside and girls yelling and screaming with their pom-poms. Almost that.

Dr. Shemp was tall and thin and tilted his head when he talked, as if his thoughts rose from his shoulder and he sucked them in and gargled them out again. He held a BlackBerry in his right hand and a clipboard tucked under his armpit. His office had old leather chairs that made saddle sounds whenever you switched your legs or changed positions. A fish tank, quiet and comforting, bubbled behind him.

"He's in rough shape," Dr. Shemp said, pushing back in his chair and putting the BlackBerry on his desk as we came in. He gestured for us to sit down. "But at this point we expect him to make it. He swallowed a lot of water and it becomes complicated with his condition. But unless he experiences a reversal of some sort, he should be fine in a few days."

"Can we see him?" I asked.

Dr. Shemp pursed his lips as if he had never been asked such a question.

"Not yet. Let him rest and we'll see how he looks in the morning. He's had a close call, you understand. He should never be allowed to attempt something like that again."

He glanced at me. Then he nodded in understanding with my mother.

"Is that it, then?" Mom asked.

"More or less," Dr. Shemp said. "Given his cystic fibrosis, he's a lucky boy. That's rough water out there. I don't think he'll suffer any long-term effects, but you can never be sure. You're from New Hampshire, correct?"

"Yes," Mom said.

"He'll have to fly, then, but I recommend you schedule an appointment for him as soon as you get back. Maybe you should call from here, or, if you like, our office can take care of that. He needs to be seen at least once more as a final check."

"Did he die?" I asked. "Was he dead?"

Dr. Shemp didn't answer.

"We understand," Mom said, reaching over to touch my

hand. "Can we at least peek in on him? We'll probably go out for something to eat, but we're going to stay here."

Dr. Shemp shrugged and said, "Wouldn't hurt, I suppose, but please don't wake him or try to communicate. Rest is what he needs right now."

We stood. Dr. Shemp stood also. He didn't extend his hand and he didn't come around the desk. We waited a second, then went out. My mother turned to me and we hugged. I felt weak and shaky.

"He's okay," she said. "He's going to be okay."

"I'm so sorry, Mom."

"I know you didn't mean it to turn out this way."

We kept hugging for a little while. When we stopped, Mom ran her hands over her eyes. She had been tearing up.

"We need to tell Ty and Little Brew," I said. "They're waiting to hear."

"Okay," Mom said, reaching out to rub my arm. "You go ahead and I'll peek in on Tommy."

I hurried to the waiting room. Ty hadn't moved, but Little Brew had figured out a way to get comfortable in the straight-backed chairs. He had his legs up and was reading a *National Geographic*. I crossed the room and smiled at Ty.

"He's going to be okay," I said. "The water got in his lungs, but he's going to be all right."

Ty stood and hugged me. Little Brew did, too. Then Ty

seemed to lose all strength and sat back down. He covered his face with his hands.

"I thought I'd killed the kid," he said from under his fingers. "I can't believe it."

"He's okay," I said and put my hand on his shoulder. "Tommy's a fighter."

"Snow Pony," Little Brew said, making his voice funny.

"Snow Pony," I said.

"I can't believe it," Ty said again. "I would never have forgiven myself."

"I guess we were nuts to let him try it," I said. "I don't know what we were thinking. We were crazy."

"We were thinking he wanted a charge," Little Brew said, his voice level. "You can't go blaming yourself when things don't turn out the way you want them to. He was stoked to do it. He didn't hesitate."

"I know," I said, "but we should have known better. I should have known better."

Ty stood back up.

"Can we see him?" he asked.

"Tomorrow," I said. "The doctor says he needs complete rest. Mom is looking in on him now."

Ty hugged me again, hard. Then I hugged Little Brew, who held on to me. The warmth of his body became the center of almost everything and I didn't want to let him go. He kissed my cheek and pulled me closer. We had been through too much in too short a time. We held each other in the middle of the waiting room. Over his shoulder I saw a light rain begin to fall in the parking lot.

TOMMY SHARK FACT #10: Tommy found a video on YouTube of a surfer in Australia being attacked by two great white sharks. He has watched it so often that he can do the play-by-play of the attack without even glancing at the video. An Italian tourist happened to be filming the surfers when a great white rose on top of a wave, grabbed a whole surfboard, and tossed it backward into the trough or valley created before the next wave. What astonished Tommy and other researchers was that the whites seemed to cooperate: a second great white was waiting in the trough. The surfer sustained a bite on his left arm, but it wasn't critical. The sharks seemed to recognize that a human is not their preferred mammal. They disappeared and the surfer made it to shore without further injury. Authorities closed the beach for a couple days, then reopened it. The YouTube video appeared on something called SharkWatch. Tommy receives e-mail alerts from a dozen shark Web sites and is a subscriber to the International Shark Attack File, a database in Florida that records and analyzes shark attacks around the world.

Tommy also tracks accounts of people feeling "sharky" or "predator-aware" just before being attacked or approached by a great white. He says that if he had the chance to research things, he might concentrate on that. According to him, the warning prickle we get along the neck may be one of our oldest, most instinctive reactions. He tells the story—from *The Devil's Teeth*, his favorite book—about an urchin diver named Joe Burke who was stalked by an enormous female great white off the Farallones. The female approached and showed aggressive interest, but what Burke later reported was a sense of cunning. The shark would disappear, then try to sneak up on Burke. Burke hid out against a pile of rocks on the bottom of the sea, but each time he left the rocks the shark reappeared. It unnerved Burke not only because this went on and on, but because the shark seemed to be enjoying it. Finally becoming nervous about his air supply, Burke climbed into his urchin basket and signaled to his partner on deck to haul him up. As he rose through the water, the shark circled, looking, so it seemed to Burke, for a way to ambush him. Burke felt connected to the shark in a prey-predator minuet, and it surprised him to discover that he knew where the shark was likely to appear an instant before she did.

● ● ●

I kissed Tommy's forehead. He didn't wake. My mom sat on a small chair next to the bed. The medical staff had taped a ventilator into Tommy's mouth. The ventilator made a small wheezing sound as it breathed with Tommy. I looked over at my mom.

What we both understood, I think, was that we would meet again like this. We knew it. The day would come when we would stand on either side of a hospital bed, Tommy between us, and that would be a different day. That would be a day without end, a day of losing Tommy, and the look that passed between us communicated that as surely as if we spoke it aloud. I watched my mom's eyes fill and for a second I imagined what it must have been like when the doctors first delivered the news about Tommy. The world had to change the minute she learned he had CF, and she had watched the symptoms progress. And since then the world had never come back to level for my mom.

Our eyes stayed on one another's for a ten count, then whatever had passed between us disappeared.

"Hungry?" my mother asked.

"Starving," I said.

"So that was the famous Ty Barry?" Mom asked, a menu spread out in front of her. "He's a handsome boy. And his brother is an absolute knockout. He's movie star material. I'm sure you didn't notice, though."

I smiled. She smiled, too.

We sat in a diner somewhere north of Redwood City. It

was the first place we came to when we drove away from the hospital in her rental. According to the back of the menu, the owners of the diner had bought it from somewhere in Indiana and had it reset out in California. They had aimed for authenticity, but they had tried so hard to get all the details correct that it seemed phony in its accuracy. The diner's name was Calamity Jane's. It had a lot of air-conditioning.

"Ty Barry was the guy who was attacked by a great white," I said. "He was on a surfboard."

"Some kind of hero to Tommy. I know about him."

She looked for the waitress, who was busy delivering food to another booth. Mom turned her attention back to the menu. She liked eating out. She always studied the menu, but never ordered anything exotic.

"Ty's been terrific to Tommy," I said. "He admires him. He's not just stringing him along. He likes Tommy."

"Why wouldn't he?" Mom asked.

She caught the waitress's eye and the frazzled waitress raised a finger to say one minute. A page of her order book hung outside the pocket of her apron and flapped whenever she moved quickly.

"Tommy doesn't have any friends, Mom," I said. "Kids his age just see a scrawny little egghead. They call him E.T. They don't have the patience they need to get to know him."

"He's got some friends. He's friends with Larry Feingold."

"Larry's a loser, Mom. He's a Dungeons and Dragons geek. Tommy doesn't even like playing with him. With Ty and Little Brew, Tommy feels like he belongs to a group. They call him Snow Pony."

"Snow Pony?"

I decided I couldn't quite explain it. I also knew Mom wasn't going to see it my way, exactly. She was hungry and wanted the waitress and it annoyed her to have to wait. Things my mom didn't want to look at closely had a way of glancing off her. Sometimes she reminded me of a snowplow, sharp and pointed, with curls of snow on either side of her. She didn't mean to ignore things around her, but she was too intent on driving ahead to see how she affected people. And right now she wanted to eat.

Finally the waitress came over and took our order. We split fries, as we usually did, and we each ordered a hamburger. Mom checked her cell phone. I sat and looked out the window. When she clicked the phone closed she turned to face me.

"I called Mr. Cotter," she said. "He's looking into whether the foundation can cover the hospital bills. If they can't, we're screwed."

"I'm sorry, Mom," I said.

She let some air out of her lips and stared at me. Then she took the saltshaker and spilled a little salt onto the table, and tried to make the shaker stand on its edge in the grains. It was tricky, but after a while she did it. She kept her eyes on the saltshaker when she spoke next.

"I know you don't think I'm much of a mother," she said and held up her hand before I could interrupt. "Don't deny it, it's okay. You think I'm overly interested in men and that I need men around me no matter what. I know what you and Tommy say about me. I'm not dumb or deaf."

I didn't answer. She looked at me quickly, then looked back at the saltshaker.

"I know," she said. "And you're right. Mostly you're right. I do need men around. I always have. I don't like it about myself. I know it's destructive a lot of the time. On the other hand, you probably don't keep track of things like I do, but I've gone years with no one around. When you were little, it was just you, me, and Tommy. Your father left as soon as he found out Tommy had CF. You don't really know about those years, Bee."

"It's okay, Mom," I said. "We don't have to go into it all."

"No," she said, "you should know about things. About me."

"I'm not judging you, Mom."

"Sure you are," she said, looking up again from the salt-shaker. "Everyone judges people. That's what humans do. It's supposed to be a survival technique. We have to judge people to know if we can trust them and if we can count on them to help us. It's a tribal thing. At least, that's what I read."

I kept quiet. I didn't want to interrupt her.

"Anyway, your dad leaves and I'm in a small New Hampshire town with two kids, one of them with CF and huge medical bills. That's a lot to handle. If you work, then you have to find someone to take care of your kids. If you find decent child care, it eats up all your money, so, in the end, you're working so a stranger stays at home with your children. Your grandparents—well, you know them. My father never cared for me. He just plain didn't like me, really. He always thought I was trashy and maybe I was. He saw the breakup of my marriage as confirmation that he had been right about me. And my mother is a mouse and couldn't squeak about boo. So, yes, I've probably been looking for some sort of daddy approval. I've read enough self-help books to know that."

The waitress came and put our burgers down. Mom squirted ketchup on her corner of the fries. I ate a couple while she prepped her burger with mustard and ketchup. It was one of my strange quirks that I never put condiments on anything I ate, so Mom didn't offer any to me. She finally plucked the saltshaker off the grains and shook some on her side of the fries.

"Is this weirding you out?" she asked. "This stuff about your dad and all?"

I shook my head. I had never heard her be so frank.

"Given what happened today," she said, "it makes sense to talk. I feel like talking, anyway. I'm not trying to make excuses; I'm just trying to shed a little light on things. And we both saw how easily things can slip away. We almost lost Tommy."

I nodded.

"That's pretty much everything," she said. "I figured it needed to be said. It probably needed to be said a long time ago."

"Can I ask something, then? If we're being honest?"

"Sure."

"Why do you keep dating guys you know are going to be such losers in the end?"

She thought about it for a second, then shook her head as much for herself as for me.

"I don't know that," she said, lifting a fry and eating it with ketchup. "Or I talk myself into thinking they're cute or charming. Everyone has some trait that's worthwhile. I try to see that. And I get lonely, Bee. Sometimes it's enough just to have someone else in the boat with you, if you know what I mean."

"I guess so," I said. "I understand that."

She looked at me. She hadn't taken a bite of her hamburger.

"It's not that I don't love you. You and Tommy," she said.

"It's not either-or. It's not guys or you two. It's not a contest."

"But you didn't come home the other night," I said. "We're out here for Tommy. It's Tommy's trip."

"I know. I was wrong about that and I'll apologize to him. And I'm apologizing to you. It felt like a vacation to me and I went with it. That was wrong. I don't always make good choices, which you already know."

"Tommy thinks it's bizarre when you stay out."

She nodded.

"I do, too," I said. "For the record."

She nodded again.

She picked up her hamburger and waited for me to pick up mine. Then she did something she hadn't done in years. She held the burger just in front of her mouth and put out her pinkies. The rule was, you could be a complete pig if you held out your pinkies, because that way you were ladylike while still biting off huge chunks of a sandwich or ice cream.

I held up my hamburger and put my pinkies out. We smiled and bit.

TUESDAY

Tommy finally came to that night. I was the only one awake.

I'd been sleeping in a chair pulled against the edge of the bed so that I could put my legs up. Mom slept near Tommy's head. Being closer, she should have been the one to wake up, but when I opened my eyes, they met Tommy's. For a second, I thought he had died. He looked white and gaunt and his eyes didn't blink. I didn't move. I watched him for a long time, our eyes still locked, until finally he blinked and I knew he wasn't dead. I stood and went around the other side of the bed, away from Mom, and I bent close to Tommy.

He couldn't speak because of the respirator. I reached down and took his hand. I squeezed and he tried to squeeze back, but his hand felt weak.

"You okay, Tommy?"

He nodded as much as he could.

"Mom's right here. Ty and Little Brew are coming to-morrow. You're going to be all right. You just swallowed water. A lot of water."

He nodded again.

"I saw a shark," I said. "On the way in. It passed right under us. It was a great white."

He nodded a third time.

I didn't say anything else for a while. I stayed near him and watched. His eyes closed for a bit, but then he opened them again. I went through our checklist of signals to make sure he could breathe and that everything was okay. Near the end, Mom woke up and kissed Tommy's fore-head. She pushed his hair back off his head and checked for fever with her lips.

"He's a little warm," she said to me. "Are you warm, Tommy?"

He shook his head an inch.

"You feel a little warm. I'm going to ask the nurse to step in. Do you feel okay otherwise?"

"I went through the checklist with him," I said.

"Do you feel okay?" she asked anyway.

He nodded.

"We don't want fever on top of everything else," Mom said, then got a look of mischief on her face. "We're not even supposed to be here. We snuck in. But I'm going to get a nurse."

She kissed him again, then stepped out. I held Tommy's hand. The respirator pushed his chest full, then let it seep down again. His chest moved like a cat crawling under a quilt.

"You were a gnarly surfer," I told him.

His lips curled into a faint smile. And he squeezed my hand.

Mr. Cotter showed up at dawn.

It was strange to see him. He looked familiar, but I couldn't place him for a few seconds. Probably I was tired. He ducked into the doorway and stood for a moment, letting his eyes adjust. I stood, but he gestured for me to stay seated.

"How is he?" he whispered.

"He's going to be fine," I said.

"Good, good, good," he said and took a few steps toward the end of the bed.

He smiled at Tommy. I realized that in the dimness, Mr. Cotter couldn't really see if Tommy was awake or not.

"Surfing, eh?" he asked, smiling at me.

"Yes, sir," I said.

"Well, I guess no harm then," he said. "It's something he'll remember."

"He wanted to try it—it meant a lot to him."

Mr. Cotter nodded.

"Is your mother around?" he asked. "I need to chat with her about some financial things."

"She went to the ladies'," I told him. "She should be right back."

"I guess," Mr. Cotter said, "the shark outing we went on was a bit disappointing to your brother."

"You tried," I said. "It must be hard when you don't know the person. Tommy is way into sharks."

"I know." He sighed. "I felt bad about that. It was the best plan we had, though."

"He appreciated it, believe me," I said. "And we did see a shark."

"That's true," Mr. Cotter agreed. "Not everyone can say that."

Mom came back then. They exchanged pleasantries, and then Mr. Cotter asked if she would mind stepping outside into the waiting room. Right after they left, a nurse and doctor came in and removed the respirator from Tommy's mouth. He had tape marks around his lips and a few gummy pieces still stuck there. The nurse used a cloth dabbed with alcohol to remove them. Tommy made a face like a little kid getting his mouth wiped down after supper.

He went right back to sleep, which surprised me. I don't know what I expected. I guess I wanted him to wake up and say everything was okay, but it dawned on me that it probably wasn't that easy for him. He still looked tired and drawn, and when he inhaled, his lungs made scuba-diver sounds.

Mom came back and told me Mr. Cotter had said good-bye and promised to look us up if he came to New Hampshire.

"He was very generous," she said, tapping her purse and sitting near Tommy's head again. "We should be fine. The foundation spoke to the airline and we got a credit and we can leave tomorrow night. Tommy should be able to travel by then."

"Good, Mom," I said. "I'm glad. I'm sorry about all that stuff."

"Tommy was still under the Blue Moon Foundation's insurance policy. It stands to reason they have a good one."

"Stands to reason," I repeated.

After that Mom worked on a Sudoku puzzle book. I felt restless, so I went to the waiting area and flipped through an issue of *US Weekly*. It seemed crazy under the circumstances to care about what starlet had lost weight, or who had a baby bump, or what so-and-so had worn to a film opening. After a few pages I grew impatient and put it aside. Then my attention wandered to the television in the far corner of the room, where people in a show wore helmets and jumpsuits and safety glasses and kept falling and stumbling over ridiculous obstacles. They got out of breath immediately. It turned my stomach to see it—it was supposed to be funny but it made me angry. I thought of Tommy and what he went through every day, and playing at suffering and making a big deal of a game show seemed sickening. Then I don't know what happened. I started crying hard, blubbering, and I put my hands over my face. I cried with my shoulders heaving backward and forward, and in the corner the television continued on. Part of me understood I was experiencing post-shock syndrome. But I was also crying because I'd witnessed how things could change so suddenly, and it gave my heart a twist to remember that.

I cried for a while. A few people came by but they probably figured I had lost someone, or gotten some hard news, and they didn't stop and they didn't really look at me. Once I felt cried out, I went into the bathroom and washed my face and combed my fingers through my hair. When I came out, Little Brew and Ty were walking through the waiting area with the shark-bitten surfboard between them.

"Guys," I said and they turned and smiled. "What are you doing awake so early?"

"Came to see Snow Pony," Little Brew said.

He came over and kissed me. It was a bright, happy kiss and I felt better instantly.

"And we brought this," Ty said, wiggling the board. "We thought it might cheer him up."

"And this," Little Brew said, holding up a plastic grocery bag. "We have some mad footage in here."

"You won't believe it," Ty said.

Seeing them lifted my spirits. It made everyone feel better, because as they carried the board through the halls, people stopped, puzzled, until Ty and Little Brew pointed out the shark bite. Then more people came forward and touched the board and it took us a few minutes to make it down the hallway, because everyone wanted to know more about it. By the time we rounded the corner into Tommy's room, he was awake and sitting up. He still looked tired and shaky, but he lit up when Ty and Little Brew plopped the board against the foot of the bed. Even my mom stood and smiled. It was good to have healthy boys around, boys who glowed with sun and salt and all that fresh air.

Mom hugged them this time. It was a nice gesture and I could tell she meant it. Then Ty and Little Brew sat down on Tommy's bed. They didn't bother with a bunch of questions about Tommy's condition.

"What are you guys doing here?" Tommy asked. "Don't you have school, L.B.?"

"We're checking on you first, Snow Pony," Little Brew said. "Big bro is making you a present of that board."

Tommy's eyes widened as he looked at Ty. "Are you kidding?"

"I've got to be done with it," Ty said. "I've held on to it too long. You keep it for a while. If I want it back, I know where to find you."

"You serious?" Tommy asked.

Ty nodded. Tommy tried to do some ridiculous handshake routine with them. They had showed it to him once, and he had flubbed it even then, but they went along with it. Then he made them carry the board over to the side of the bed so that he could touch it. He explained the story to my mom, who maybe finally got a glimpse of what sharks could do. She ran her fingers over the board and let Tommy go sharky on her. He told her the entire Ty-Barry-got-hit-off-the-board story. Ty simply listened.

"We have something else," Little Brew said when Tommy finished. "Check this out."

"I'm going to close the blinds so we can see better," Ty said.

He fussed with the blinds and the room went dim. We all grouped around the head of the bed with Tommy in the center. Little Brew had to lie across Tommy's legs so that we could all see the screen, a tiny flip-out deal that came off the side of the recorder.

Little Brew hit Play and we squinted at the screen: it was the surf footage that Ollie had shot. It jumped around a good deal, but eventually I made out the group of surfers sitting beyond the breakers and watching the waves. Then I saw Willy take off, his ride perfect, which then blended into Ty's solo ride. Ollie had done a good job bleeding different lines together, but it also made it a tiny bit confusing. The film only made complete sense when I saw myself jump off the back of the Jet Ski. Ollie focused in on me as I climbed onto Ty's board, and then he cut to us flying down the face of the wave. It looked amazing. He ran it in slow motion so that we could see every detail, and I had to admit my ride looked pretty daring. The wave curled above us like a flyswatter, and then it came down and swamped us. I saw myself smiling, a deep, happy smile, and I didn't say it aloud, but I liked how I looked.

"Look at Bee's Knees," Tommy said. "She's a rad surfing babe."

I smiled at Tommy and he smiled back. I had never seen him so happy.

The footage showed Ty and Tommy's run, too. I winced a little when the wave dumped them, but Little Brew backed it up and slowed it down and we watched it four or five times. Each time I saw Tommy's face jammed with a full-on smile, his body tiny against Ty's, his arms brittle sticks. On the last run, though, Little Brew looked up at Ty and laughed.

"I knew they wouldn't see it," Little Brew said.

"See what?" Mom asked.

"The shark fin."

"*Maybe* a shark fin," Ty corrected. "It's hard to tell."

"What are you talking about?" I asked.

They showed us. It took a lot of back-and-forthing to get the scene they wanted, but finally they froze the camera on the shot of Tommy and Ty getting crushed by the wave. I examined the picture but I didn't see anything. Mom leaned closer and nodded. Tommy didn't see anything, either.

"I didn't notice it at first," Little Brew said. "Ollie spotted it when he edited the shoot. Right there, in the corner."

Tommy did his best to lean forward.

"I see it now," he said. "Wow! That thing is huge."

He pointed. I leaned closer and then I saw it, too. To say it was a fin would be an overstatement. It was a tiny black point, maybe a piece of driftwood, maybe a strange break in the waves. It looked dark, though, and angled, as if the shark had been pointed more or less toward Tommy and Ty. If it had been a shark, then it probably went under them somehow, maybe losing their outline in the churning break. I wasn't ready to go that far, but it didn't matter.

Tommy, I could tell, had already bought the whole thing. He kept turning to look at me, his eyes wide, his mouth open. He had been in the water with a great white. That was all that mattered.

"That's a great white," he said. "Must be the same one you saw, Bee."

"Probably," Little Brew said, though I couldn't tell if he believed it. "It's the only thing that makes sense."

"So you're saying," my mom said, her voice happy and tight, her hand ruffling Tommy's hair, "that you put my son into the water with a great white shark?"

"And your daughter," I added.

"I can't believe it," Tommy said, as excited as I had ever seen him. "I cannot freaking believe it."

"Not only that," Little Brew said, "that shark was hunting you."

"Wanted some Tommy sushi," Ty said. "A little Snow Pony roll."

Tommy could hardly contain himself. He made a little wiggle motion on the bed. I had only seen him do that once or twice in his life.

"It must have been cruising around," Tommy said, his breath wheezy. "Bee's Knees saw it, too. It looks like it was coming right at us."

"I'll never go into the water again," Mom said, playing her role up a little.

"It is *sooooo* rare," Tommy said. "I mean, one in about one hundred million."

"You have a better chance of winning the lottery," Ty said. "Trust me, I know."

After that, Tommy made them run the footage back and forth about a thousand times. My mom asked me to come help her and we went and ordered two pizzas for breakfast from the small shop in the hospital. We got sodas, too. When we carried everything back, a few of the nurses had come in to look at the footage. Tommy was crazy happy. One of the nurses said they should send the footage to the local news program. Little Brew agreed, except he said Ollie had already posted it to YouTube.

"Snow Pony is swimming with the man," Little Brew said, his voice revving Tommy up again. "That shark was looking for you, buddy."

"You have some weird shark mojo," Tommy told Ty. "You're a shark magnet."

"Bee said it was big, too," Little Brew said. "Like triple the Jet Ski at least."

We had pizza and watched some more footage. Ollie had some earlier filming spliced in and the boys surfed beautifully, scraping down the side of a few huge sets. The new segment wasn't accompanied by music, but the old video had music by Anthrax, a mega-hard-rock band that made the entire thing feel a little frantic. Ollie cut in some

Hawaiian music, too, and that made the surf scenes seem surreal and funny after all the crash-metal stuff. It was pretty good filmmaking. Ollie had a nice eye and the surf footage was compelling all on its own.

"You'll send me all the footage, right?" Tommy asked when Ty and Little Brew were getting ready to leave. They had each eaten three slices of pizza.

"Sure, of course," Ty said. "We'll mail it this week."

"You're like a YouTube star," Little Brew said. "It's already going viral."

Tommy got quiet. It was clear he didn't want them to go. I didn't want them to go, either. But the doctors had already said he could leave the hospital that afternoon. My mom, to her credit, tried to make the goodbye smooth while the guys did a handshake-shoulder-bump-thing with Tommy. It didn't make sense to delay any longer. We were heading back to San Francisco once Tommy got released.

"I know you guys put yourselves out for me," Tommy said, his voice knotty with breath and lung gunk. "I want you to know I appreciate it."

"No problem," Ty said. "I'm glad I finally got to meet you."

"This was the best time of my life," Tommy said the way only he could say it, all heart and vulnerability.

"I'll walk you out," I said. "I'd like to get some air, anyway."

They hugged Tommy one last time. Then they hugged Mom. Ty touched the surfboard as he went out. I couldn't quite read his expression. Cali boys. Tommy's best friends. Maybe Tommy's only friends.

"I made this for you," Little Brew said as we stood in front of the hospital.

He handed me a hemp necklace with a cowry shell in the center and two blue-gray beads on each side.

"So that you remember California," he said.

"I'll remember California."

"And me, I hope."

"And you," I said. "You most of all."

I held the necklace up to my throat and turned around. Little Brew attached the clasp. His hands trailed on my neck as I turned back to face him.

"Thank you," I said. "Thanks for everything."

"I'm glad we met, Bee. Maybe I'll come out to New Hampshire one of these days. I have an uncle who lives in Boston."

"That would be great," I said. "And maybe I could come out here sometime."

He smiled. "And we can e-mail."

He pulled me closer and we kissed. It was a perfect kiss—tender, passionate, and lingering. As we came apart, I still couldn't quite believe that this beautiful boy liked me.

I waved to Ty. He had the van running. He waved back. Little Brew trotted around the front of the van and climbed into the passenger side. They had two surfboards secured to the top. As they pulled away, Little Brew leaned across Ty and shouted something. I didn't quite catch what he said. I waved goodbye, the sun bright in my eyes. It was only after they had put on their blinker and slid off into the traffic that I pieced together what Little Brew had said.

Look up, he had shouted, reminding me of the stars.

WEDNESDAY

A shark killed a swimmer the next morning. It happened miles away, much farther south, the first shark-attack death off San Diego in more than half a century. Experts blamed it on a great white. A group of marathon swimmers had been out for an early training swim about a hundred yards off a San Diego beach when the last swimmer got knocked into the air and yelled, "Shark!"

Then he went under. By the time two swimmers came back and helped him to the beach, blood had already geysered out of his leg. One of the men said he had felt the blood, warmer than the water, pouring past him as it jetted from his friend's body. The shark, they said, did not re-appear, although they expected a second attack at any moment.

They pulled the victim to a rocky cove and someone ran for the lifeguards, who returned in a beach cart and took the injured man to get help. By that time, unfortunately, the man had already died from a severed artery in his leg. The authorities closed the beach and sent out choppers to scout the area for the shark. An alert went up and down the coastline, because great whites were known to patrol the area. Most experts concluded that the shark had seen the silhouette of the swimmer and had mistaken him for a seal. Typical of a great white attack, the shark had picked the trailing member of the group and had come up at a forty-five- to ninety-degree angle. As powerful as a great white can be, it still relies on ambush.

Standing in front of breaking surf, the television reporter explained how exceedingly rare such an attack was. He was a young guy with an open collar. He kept turning to look over his shoulder at the water, as if he could make a shark appear. At the same time he seemed glad to be on solid land. The wind pushed his hair around.

We watched the report on an airport television. It was after we had checked the surfboard, which Tommy and I had carried between us. People had come over to ask about the bite mark. Tommy was crazy proud to show it off and tell them Ty's story. Invariably, everyone touched the board. The whole thing tied together. Tommy and Ty and sharks in the water. It was strange that way.

We checked the surfboard only after Tommy made the baggage staff wrap it with foam padding. He was determined not to let the board get dinged.

"Okay," he said when it was good and tight.

The baggage lady needed help from another person to put the surfboard on the conveyor belt. Then it disappeared through a black rubber-curtained hatch.

My mom checked us in and we had about an hour and a half to kill before our flight, so we went to an airport restaurant and had chicken sandwiches. We had eaten about half of our meal when the shark-attack report came on for what was probably a second or third time that day. When Mom saw Tommy and me staring at the TV, she turned and watched, too.

"Oh, goodness," Mom said, her voice tight, "can that be the same shark?"

"Could be," Tommy said, his jaw set. "No way to know."

"Could it get that far that fast?" Mom asked.

"Probably not," Tommy said. "Probably it's all just a coincidence. It's weird, though. I wonder if Ty and Little Brew have heard about it."

I moved my eyes back and forth between Tommy and the television. I could tell that this attack was hitting him differently than the ones that had come before. This one wasn't theoretical. He had been in the ocean with a shark, and in rough water, at that, the bottom a million miles below, the big, scary thing patrolling around his legs. He had seen a shark, maybe, pointed toward him. So he stopped eating as he watched the television. When the report ended, he shook his head.

"That's just bizarre," he said. "Especially after what happened to us."

"It could have been either of you two," Mom said. "That's what hits me."

"It's their season," he said. "They have to put on weight or they won't survive. You can't blame them. They're just doing what they need to do."

"But to possibly be eaten . . . ," Mom said.

"Yes, can you imagine how scared the swimmer must have been?" I asked.

"The sharks have a right to exist, too," Tommy said, his eyes a little glassy. "When you go into the ocean, you go into their world. They don't come on land and get us. And when it's your time to go, it's your time to go."

Mom looked at me. I knew she suspected that Tommy was talking about himself. I wondered that, too.

He didn't talk any more and we didn't see another report about the attack.

"You tired?" I asked Tommy as the plane flew somewhere over the Midwest.

It was dark outside. Mom sat across the aisle. This time she hadn't flirted with anyone. She did her Sudoku puzzles until Nebraska, then fell asleep. The puzzle book lay open on her belly.

Tommy didn't answer. He sat by the window, looking out. The light on the top of the wing sometimes threw shadows on him. A bag of peanuts lay scattered on the fold-down table in front of him.

"That board is going to look amazing in your room," I said. "Where are you going to put it? Over your bed might be good."

Again, he didn't respond. It wasn't like him to be blue. I put my hand on his knee and squeezed it. He looked over. His eyes were filled with tears.

"What is it?" I asked him, surprised.

"It's just that it's all done now. I don't have it to look forward to anymore."

"There'll be other things," I said. "Plenty of things."

"Maybe. It just feels funny right now."

He twisted toward the window so that he wouldn't have to look at me. I didn't push it; he was rarely moody. He ate a couple of peanuts.

"Thanks for everything you did, Bee," he said, turning to me after a while. "No one else would have understood."

"You're my brother and I love you," I said. "I'd do whatever I could for you."

"Still, though. You never ask for anything for yourself. Someday I'd like to do something for you."

"You do plenty for me, Tommy."

"I mean like an adventure. Like what we just had. You get kind of lost in the shuffle because everyone pays attention to me. Because of the CF."

"I think I had my own adventure," I said. "Truly."

"You mean Little Brew?"

Tommy wiggled his eyebrows. I shoved my shoulder into his.

"Little Brew wouldn't have given you that necklace if he didn't like you," Tommy said. "He's not phony. Ty told me Little Brew never goes after a girl."

"Girls go after him, I bet."

Tommy laughed. "Probably if they're not blind," he said. "He's golden."

"You're golden, too, Bee. Will you guys e-mail?"

"Absolutely. And I hope we see each other again."

"Just say you will and you will. I wanted to see a shark and I did. If you wish for something, it stands a chance of happening."

Later on Tommy sighed and said he didn't really know why he loved sharks, but that it didn't matter. You didn't always have to explain why you loved something. Love was a thing that swam beneath you, kind of like a shark, and you wouldn't want the world to be without it, but it could hurt, too. He said that late at night he often thinks of sharks swimming, their pectoral fins stabilizing them, their bodies perfect triangles as they soar through the water, and he sometimes finds he is looking from the shark's perspective at the water in front of him. Sometimes he feels exactly like the sharks he loves, like a thing in constant movement, always hunting, always moving forward, but the sea around him is impenetrable. Everything is shadow and light and bright things that flash and move away. He said sometimes he thinks he likes sharks because his illness made other people leery, made them afraid that what he had could pass to them somehow, and when a shark patrolled a reef or passed near a seal colony the other creatures ran not only for their lives, but because a shark was the other side of their characters. So he was not afraid of sharks, he *was* a shark, and the CF marked him among other people. That was why Ty and

Little Brew meant so much. That was why one day, filled all the way up, meant so much to him. In the California sun he had shed his sharkness, left it for a moment, and he had risen up, a surfer, a boy again, triumphant despite everything.

That was how he said it, more or less. He said it in his Tommy way. I listened. I put my arm around him and we flew through the night, heading home to New Hampshire.

AFTERWORD

When I was in eighth grade, I came across a book about a series of shark attacks off the New Jersey coastline not far from where I grew up, and I have been a lover of shark tales ever since. Once, sitting on a jetty near Point Pleasant, New Jersey, I saw a shark following a fishing boat into port, and I was mesmerized by the fin cleaving the water, the lazy swish of the animal as the shark fed on the entrails thrown aft by the mate. Although I am not entirely proud of it, I confess I have always been drawn to accounts of sharks attacking humans. I'm not sure why I thrill to those accounts, but I know I am not alone. Many of us respond to such stories. The popularity of movies such as *Jaws* and *Open Water* and the ever-increasing viewership of the Discovery Channel's Shark Week attest to our fascination with these beautiful—and occasionally deadly—creatures of the sea.

But if we love sharks, or at least find them interesting and worthy of our observation, then it's important to remind ourselves that humans are far deadlier to sharks than the reverse. I've heard it said that the likelihood of an individual's dying by shark attack is roughly equivalent to the likelihood of death by a coconut falling on the head. While it's true that our increased recreation in the sea—skin diving, distance swimming, surfing, and kayaking—puts us more consistently in the sharks' path, sharks suffer much more from our predation than we do from theirs. Caught on long fishing lines—by some estimates more than six hundred every minute—killed for sport and to satisfy the demand for shark-fin soup, the world's shark population has been heavily depleted. Though we marvel at pictures of great whites breaching off the coast of South Africa as they attack seals on the sea's surface, we pay little attention to the daily decimation visited by humans on sharks. The story behind Shark Week, in other words, is far grimmer than we might like to admit.

It's my hope that *Wish* reminds us of our obligation to the animals around us, especially, in this instance, to sharks.

Perhaps the love and admiration Tommy brings to his study of sharks will help us to see animals on their own terms. A shark goes about a shark's business, and if that business sometimes includes a human victim, then that is regrettable but entirely understandable. Sharks are not monsters. They are our companions on this earth.

As someone once said, a world without tigers is no world at all. I think the same can be said about sharks.

ACKNOWLEDGMENTS

I am indebted to Susan Casey's fine account of her time spent near the Farallon Islands for some of the atmosphere and background of this novel. I recommend her book *The Devil's Teeth: A True Story of Obsession and Survival Among America's Great White Sharks* to anyone interested in reading more about great whites. Some of Tommy's shark facts — and his sightseeing trip to the Farallones — grew directly from my reading of Ms. Casey's work.

I am also grateful to my editor, Françoise Bui, for her excellent reading of this novel. Her comments and suggestions improved the manuscript from its original conception. Thanks, also, to my friends and agents Christina Hogrebe and Andrea Cirillo, both of whom provided insight into the characters and plot. It is a genuine pleasure to work with them.

Finally, to my wife, Wendy, who is always my first reader — thanks for everything.

ABOUT THE AUTHOR

JOSEPH MONNINGER has published eleven novels and three nonfiction books for adults, as well as two award-winning novels for young adults: *Hippie Chick*, a *Bulletin* Blue Ribbon Book, and *Baby*, an ALA-YALSA Top Ten Best Book for Young Adults. He lives in New Hampshire, where he is an English professor.